HE̶RO̶ES̶!

BOOK 2

THE MAN IN THE IRON SOCKS

OXFORD

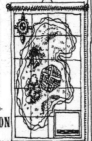

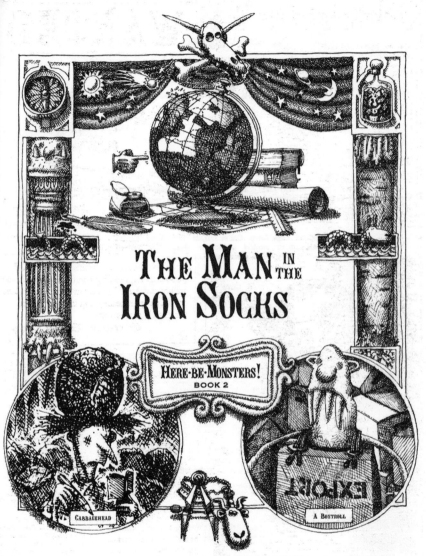

THE MAN IN THE IRON SOCKS

HERE·BE·MONSTERS!
BOOK 2

CABBAGEHEAD

A BOXTROLL

WRITTEN AND ILLUSTRATED

by Alan Snow

To Edward, and with enormous thanks
to everyone who has helped along the way

Great Clarendon Street, Oxford OX2 6DP

Oxford University Press is a department of the University of Oxford.
It furthers the University's objective of excellence in research, scholarship,
and education by publishing worldwide in

Oxford New York

Auckland Cape Town Dar es Salaam Hong Kong Karachi
Kuala Lumpur Madrid Melbourne Mexico City Nairobi
New Delhi Shanghai Taipei Toronto

With offices in

Argentina Austria Brazil Chile Czech Republic France Greece
Guatemala Hungary Italy Japan Poland Portugal Singapore
South Korea Switzerland Thailand Turkey Ukraine Vietnam

Oxford is a registered trade mark of Oxford University Press
in the UK and in certain other countries

Text and illustrations © Alan Snow 2005

The moral rights of the author have been asserted

Database right Oxford University Press (maker)

First published 2005 as part of *Here Be Monsters!*
First published in this paperback edition 2008

British Library Cataloguing in Publication Data

Data available

ISBN: 978-0-19-275541-4

1 3 5 7 9 10 8 6 4 2

Printed in Great Britain by Cox & Wyman Ltd, Reading, Berkshire.

CONTENTS

Johnson's Taxonomy
of Trolls and Creatures

Aardvark
Aardvarks are invariably the first animals listed in any alphabetical listing of creatures. Beyond this they have few attributes relevant here.

Boxtrolls
A sub-species of the common troll, they are very shy, so live inside a box. These they gather from the backs of large shops. They are somewhat troublesome creatures—as they have a passion for everything mechanical and no understanding of the concept of ownership (they steal anything which is not bolted down, and more often than not, anything which is). It is very dangerous to leave tools lying about where they might find them.

Cabbageheads
Belief has it that cabbageheads live deep underground and are the bees of the underworld. Little else is known at this time, apart from a fondness for brassicas.

Cheese
Wild English Cheeses live in bogs. This is unlike their French cousins who live in caves. They are nervous beasties, that eat grass by night, in the meadows and woodlands. They are also of very low intelligence, and are panicked by almost anything that catches them unawares. Cheeses make easy quarry for hunters, being rather easier to catch than a dead sheep.

Crow
The crow is a very intelligent bird, capable of living in many environments. Crows are known to be considerably more honest than their cousins, magpies, and enjoy a varied diet, and good company. Usually they are charming company, but should be kept from providing the entertainment. Failure to do so may result in tedium, for while intelligent, crows seem to lack taste in the choice of music, and conversational topics.

Fresh-water Sea-cow
Distant relative of the manitou. This creature inhabits the canals, and drains of certain West Country towns. A passive creature of large size, and vegetarian habits. They are very kind to their young, and make good mothers.

Grandfather (William)

Arthur's guardian and carer. Grandfather has lived underground for many years in a cave home where he pursues his interests in engineering. All the years in a damp cave have taken their toll, and he now suffers from very bad rheumatism, and a somewhat short temper.

The Man in the Iron Socks

A mysterious shadowy figure said to be much feared by the members of the now defunct Cheese Guild. He is thought to hold a dark secret as well as a large 'Walloper'. His Walloper is the major cause of fear, but he also has a sharp tongue, and a caustic line in wit. History does not relate the reasoning behind his wearing of iron socks.

The Members

Members of the secretive Ratbridge Cheese Guild, that was thought to have died out after the 'Great Cheese Crash'. It was an evil organization that rigged the cheese market, and doctored and adulterated lactose-based food stuffs.

Rabbits

Furry, jumping mammals, with a passion for tender vegetables and raising the young. Good parents, but not very bright.

Rabbit Women

Very little is known about these mythical creatures, except that they are supposed to live with rabbits, and wear clothes spun from rabbit wool.

Rats

Rats are known to be some of the most intelligent of all rodents, and to be considerably more intelligent than many humans. They are known to have a passion for travel, and be extremely adaptable. They often live in a symbiotic relationship with humans.

Trotting Badgers

Trotting badgers are some of the nastiest creatures to be found anywhere. With their foul temper, rapid speed, and razor-sharp teeth, it cannot be stressed just how unpleasant and dangerous these creatures are. It is only their disgusting stench that gives warning of their proximity, and when smelt it is often too late.

THE STORY SO FAR ...

ARTHUR ABOVE GROUND!

ARTHUR has lived all his life in the Underworld, deep below the streets of Ratbridge, with his grandfather. Now that Grandfather is too frail to leave his bed, Arthur must come above ground to forage for food to take back down below. With a great deal of care, and using the special set of wings that Grandfather has made him, he can keep out of the way of curious Ratbridge residents.

Arthur at large

THE CHEESE HUNT

BUT one day Arthur takes an extra risk. He is intrigued by the sight of a cheese hunt—which he knows has long been illegal as it is cruel to cheese—and he can't resist moving in to watch.

The huntsmen set off home with the cheese in tow

CAUGHT!

GOING too close, Arthur reveals himself and is caught by the frightening Archibald Snatcher and his band of men. Snatcher is fascinated by Arthur's wings and steals them.

Snatcher grabs the wings

Willbury with the boxtrolls and Titus the cabbagehead

A REFUGE

WITH a great deal of luck, Arthur manages to get away, and finds refuge in a strange old pet shop, with Willbury Nibble QC and the Underworld creatures that live with him.

THE PLOT THICKENS

WILLBURY promises to help Arthur get home. His boxtroll and cabbagehead friends know many ways down into the Underworld, so they can help Arthur find a way back. But when they go out they discover to their horror that all the entrances into the Underworld have been sealed up. Arthur is in despair— how will he get back and take food to Grandfather now?

A large rusty iron plate covered the hole

A SINISTER VISITOR

WILLBURY promises to help Arthur and they go back to the pet shop to think. There they have a visitor— Mr Gristle—who has brought some miniature creatures to sell them.

'I wonder if you might be interested in buying some rather small creatures'

AN OUTRAGEOUS REQUEST

INTRIGUED as he has never seen such tiny creatures before, Willbury buys a tiny boxtroll, cabbagehead, and sea-cow, but he is horrified at Gristle's repeated demands to buy the big creatures, and sends him packing.

'I do not sell friends!'

IN THE MARKET

A very strange woman

WILLBURY and Arthur next set off to look for Willbury's friend Marjorie, an inventor, who may have heard something about who has stolen Arthur's wings. On the way, they have another surprise as they come upon the bizarre Madame Froufrou in the marketplace, selling miniature creatures to the fashionable ladies of Ratbridge. Arthur thinks Madame Froufrou looks strangely familiar, but cannot think why.

MARJORIE

THEY find Marjorie, who is upset as she has invented something wonderful—too secret to tell them about —and her invention has been stolen by an unscrupulous father and son, Louis and Edward Trout.

A very upset Marjorie

'Good morning! Need any washing done?'

GONE!

TOGETHER the friends go back to the pet shop. But there a disaster awaits them. While they were out, the pet shop has been ransacked—and all the big creatures have been stolen! As they stand wondering what to do, a sailor called Kipper and a rat called Tom arrive, from the Ratbridge Nautical Laundry.

SKULDUGGERY!

TOM and Kipper tell them that some rats have gone missing from the Laundry, too—and they suspect that some shady characters from the Cheese Hall are responsible—including Snatcher and Gristle! Everyone decides they must work together to find out what is going on, and to get their friends back, and so they set off for the Nautical Laundry to make a plan . . .

'Something has got to be done!'

CABBAGEHEADS

MEANWHILE, we discover that the Underworld has started to flood. A colony of cabbageheads is forced to move to look for drier ground. But they stumble into a terrible trap . . .

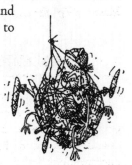

Caught in a net and collected by a group of men wearing tall hats

Willbury paused, then pulled the knob

A pair of eyes peered out

Chapter 1

THE CHEESE HALL

The door of the Cheese Hall stood at street level, and was made from very solid-looking oak. Large iron studs were fixed at regular intervals across its surface, and at head height was a metal grille that covered a small hatch. Willbury approached it rather nervously. To one side of the door frame was a metal knob shaped like a cheese. Beneath it a dirty brass plaque read 'pull'. Willbury paused, then pulled the knob.

The sound of a cheese bleat could be heard distantly through the door. Willbury raised an eyebrow. Of all the knockers and bells he had knocked, pulled, or pushed, this was certainly the strangest. Then he heard steps, the hatch flew open, and a pair of eyes peered out.

'Yes!' snapped a voice. 'What d'yer want?'

'I ... er ... would like to talk to someone,' replied Willbury.

'You buying or selling?' The voice sounded very annoyed.

Willbury thought for a moment. 'I am not really buying . . . or selling.'

'Well, you ain't no interest to us then. Now naff off!' And the hatch snapped shut.

Willbury stood for a moment, rather perplexed, then he looked back towards the pub where the others were hiding. The window of the pub had most of the crew's faces pressed hard against it. He waved at them to get them to hide properly, and they reluctantly disappeared.

The window of the pub had most of the crew's faces pressed hard against it

He turned back to the door and pulled the knob again. The bleating started but was cut short by the sound of a thump, then the hatch swung open again.

'What d'you want now?' snapped the voice.

'Would it be possible to talk to someone about cheese?' Willbury asked.

'No! Cheese is our business, and information about cheese is confidential. I told you to naff off, so go on . . . Take a walk!' The hatch slammed shut.

Willbury was left standing in the rain, staring at the door. He was not quite sure what to do. He had not expected a warm welcome, but nor had he expected this total failure. He looked up at the building. Wooden boards were nailed over most of the windows, but from between gaps in the planks several pairs of eyes were staring down at him.

'I am being watched,' he muttered. He turned and nonchalantly walked across the street and into the Nag's Head.

As soon as he walked inside he was surrounded.

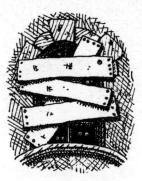

From between gaps in the planks several pairs of eyes were staring at him

'What they say then?' asked the captain.

'Not a lot!' said Willbury.

'Did you ask if they had our friends?' asked Kipper.

'I didn't really get round to that. They were not very chatty,' Willbury admitted. 'I wonder what our next step is?'

'Storm them with grappling hooks!' said a very enthusiastic Bert.

'We ain't got no grappling hooks, and anyway it looks a pretty tough building to storm,' Tom replied.

'Well, we could go back to the ship and get the cannon?' said Kipper.

'I don't think that the police are going to put up with members of the local laundry letting off cannons in the street,' said Willbury.

'I don't think that the police are going to put up with members of the local laundry letting off cannons in the street.'

'And we ain't got no gunpowder,' said Jim regretfully.

'Maybe there is another way in,' suggested Arthur.

'There is one other way in. The mice told me about it,' said Bert. 'If you look right up at the roof, you can see a pair of doors, with a crane that sticks out just above them. It's like one of them Dutch ones they use for lifting pianos into attics and the like. I don't think there is any way we can use that, as it's controlled from inside the building.'

'If you look right up at the roof, you can see a pair of doors'

One of the other rats raised his hand. 'S'cuse me, but ain't they got a sewer?'

'The mice say the Cheese Hall has got its own cesspit and well. They're not connected up to the main systems, so it's impossible to use those to get in. The place is like a fortress!' said Bert.

'Well, how are we going to find out whether they got our mates then?' asked Tom.

'How about we kidnap one of them and torture 'im!' said Jim.

'Yeah!' agreed Bert.

'I don't think that's quite the right thing to do,' said Willbury. 'I think we have no choice but to watch the place and see what happens. An opportunity may present itself.'

'Does that mean we all get to stay in the pub?' said Kipper hopefully. Tom shot him another disapproving look.

'We just need someone here where they can see the entrance. How about we rent a room and set up watch?' said Arthur.

'Sounds like a very good idea to me,' said Willbury.

'And cheaper than keeping the whole crew in the pub,' added the captain.

There was a fluttering and Mildred made her way to the front

'We could keep in touch if crows act as messengers and fly back and forth to the laundry,' said Tom.

There was a fluttering and Mildred made her way to the front.

'I would like to volunteer to act as messenger,' said Mildred.

'Thank you,' said Willbury. 'And who would like to take first watch?'

'I will,' said Arthur.

'I don't think so,' replied Willbury.

'It's not going to be dangerous just looking out of a window,' pleaded Arthur. 'And besides, it was my idea. I know I can do this, Willbury, please let me.'

'All right then, but you are only to watch. I think it best though that someone else stays with you,' said Willbury.

Kipper broke in. 'Let me and Tom look after Arthur! We won't let him get into trouble.'

'All right. But if anything happens you are just to send a message back to the laundry,' insisted Willbury. 'I want to go back with the rest of the crew to check that the little creatures are all right.'

'Me too,' said Marjorie. 'The poor little things seemed so frightened . . . '

Willbury walked over to the bar.

'Excuse me, do you have a room I can rent?' he asked the landlady.

'I am afraid we only have a small one in the attic left, as it is market day,' she answered.

'Does it have a window on the street?' asked Willbury.

'Yes. Who's it for?' she asked.

Willbury pointed out Arthur, Tom, Kipper, and Mildred. The landlady looked rather unsure. 'The crow will have to perch on the curtain rail and it will be extra if boots are worn in bed.'

'Certainly,' said Willbury, and he handed over the money.

The landlady showed Arthur, Tom, Kipper, and Mildred to the room, while Willbury, Marjorie, and the rest of the crew returned to the Nautical Laundry.

The landlady

The Nag's Head

The sign of the Nag's Head

Chapter 2

AN INCIDENT OUTSIDE THE NAG'S HEAD

Arthur, Tom, Kipper, and Mildred returned downstairs to the bar and ordered some food. Then they settled at a table in the window of the bar. The rain fell, and slowly it grew dark outside.

By ten o'clock they retired to the attic, having finished fourteen games of Old Maid, twenty-seven games of dominoes, and building a large castle from the crusts of toasted sandwiches.

A large castle from the crusts of toasted sandwiches

Mildred perched on the curtain pole and went to sleep

'Shall I light a candle?' asked Arthur.

'No,' said Tom. 'Best not to. But why don't you open the window, then we will be able to hear if anything is happening, and we'll be able to put our feet up.'

Arthur opened the window and looked down. Nothing was happening. Tom and Kipper took one of the two single beds and lay down. Mildred perched on the curtain pole and went to sleep. Arthur stood by the window watching. Soon all he could hear was the rain, and Kipper snoring.

Arthur took out his doll, and quietly wound it up.

When it was ready, Arthur whispered, 'Grandfather. It's Arthur! Are you still awake?'

A sleepy voice broke through the crackling. 'Yes, Arthur.'

'How are you?' Arthur asked.

'I could be better,' came the reply. 'It is getting very damp down here. It's playing havoc with my rheumatism. The boxtrolls don't seem to be keeping up with the maintenance. But maybe I am just getting old and grumpy.'

'You stay in bed and keep warm.'

'What about you, Arthur? What's happening up there?' Grandfather asked.

Arthur told him everything that had happened. When he had finished his grandfather remained silent.

'Grandfather . . . Grandfather . . . Are you still there?' Arthur called.

Then his grandfather spoke. There was no longer any trace of sleepiness in his voice. 'Listen to me, Arthur. You are not to do anything rash. That is an order! I don't want you to do anything but watch. Mr Archibald Snatcher is a very dangerous man!'

'You know him?' asked Arthur.

'Oh yes . . . I know him . . . ' Grandfather's voice sounded angry. 'And he is the reason we live down here!'

'What!' Arthur was shocked.

'Trust me, Arthur. Stay well away from that man.'

'But what did he . . . ' Arthur broke off as there was a noise from the street below. 'Sorry, Grandfather . . . but something is happening.' Arthur peered out of the window. Below in the street a shaft of light fell from the open door of the Cheese Hall. Slowly a procession of horses and riders were making their way out into the street. It was the hunt.

'I've got to go, Grandfather.'

'Arthur! Arthur! Be careful!' Grandfather called.

'I will be. Don't worry. I'll talk to you later.'

The doll fell silent, and Arthur tucked it under his suit. Then he shook Kipper and Tom awake.

'Quick! It's the cheese hunt. They're coming out of the hall!' he whispered.

Kipper, Arthur, and Tom at the attic window

Kipper and Arthur went to the window and looked down.

'It's them I had the run in with,' said Arthur. 'But I can't see him!'

'Who do you mean?' asked Kipper.

'Snatcher!' answered Arthur.

Tom scrabbled up onto the windowsill and looked out. There was a yapping and howling as the hounds appeared. A mild panic broke out amongst the 'horses', as they did their best to avoid the hounds.

'Do you think we should send a message to the laundry?' asked Arthur.

'Yes, but let's just wait a few minutes to see what happens,' said Tom. 'Then we might be able to send more useful information.'

A large figure appeared from the door of the Cheese Hall, and the noise in the street subsided. It was Snatcher.

A riderless 'horse' walked forward, and one of the members crouched down to form a step for his leader. Snatcher closed the door, stood on the 'step', and climbed onto his mount. The hunt crowded around Snatcher, who started talking to his men. Try as they might, Arthur, Tom and Kipper could not make out his words.

A large figure appeared from the door of the Cheese Hall

'Let's get downstairs and see what Snatcher's saying,' said Tom. 'Kipper, wake up Mildred.'

Kipper reached up and poked the crow. There was a fluttering, and Mildred settled on his shoulder.

Arthur led the way downstairs. When they reached the front door, he lifted the latch very slowly and opened the door a few inches, careful not to make a sound. They could hear Snatcher addressing the group.

Snatcher closed the door, stood on the 'step', and climbed onto his mount

'The Great One is growing ever greater, and his needs must be met. We must get all the cheese we can tonight. I don't want no slacking. Anybody I catch not pulling their weight . . . ' he paused ' . . . may find themselves in "reduced circumstances" . . . Get my drift?' Snatcher's oily voice floated over the crowd.

'How much longer is we going to have to go hunting for the Great One?' came a voice.

'The time is very near! Soon we will free the Great One, and revenge will be ours!'

Evil chuckling filled the street. A shiver ran down Arthur's spine. What were these men plotting? Snatcher raised a hand.

'Quiet, my boys!' said Snatcher and the hunt calmed down. ''Tis time to wend our way.'

Snatcher kicked his horse and led off down the street. The hunt followed.

'Quick!' said Arthur. 'Let's follow them!'

'OK. Mildred, can you go back to the laundry and tell them about the hunt,' asked Tom.

As the hunt was disappearing down the street, Arthur, Tom, Kipper, and Mildred slipped out of the Nag's Head. There was a quiet flapping as Mildred disappeared. Under the cover of the shadows they began to follow the hunt down the street. Suddenly there was a shout.

'Hunt! Whoa! I've forgot me hornswoggle!' It was Snatcher.

The hunt making off down the street

'Quick!' said Tom as he looked about. 'Hide before he comes back.'

Kipper pointed back towards an alley. They turned, ran past the Cheese Hall, and into the alley.

Soon they could hear a 'horse' coming up the street. Arthur sneaked a look. Snatcher dismounted and headed for the door of the Cheese Hall. He unlocked it and disappeared inside.

Arthur sneaked a look

'Tom!' Arthur whispered. 'Can you distract the horse? I am going to see if I can get inside the Cheese Hall.'

Tom looked worried. 'It's not safe, Arthur!'

'I know. But it may be our only chance to get our friends back,' replied Arthur.

'I don't think we should let you go in there,' Kipper said, looking worried.

'Come on! There's no time to argue. I have to do this,' replied Arthur.

Tom and Kipper looked at each other for a moment, and then Tom nodded. He scuttled silently towards the 'horse', and made a very convincing bark. The 'horse' started, then Tom jumped as high as he could and bit one of the 'legs'.

'AAAAAAAH! Blinkin' hound!' came a shout from the horse, and it made off down the street.

Tom waved to Arthur, who took a last glance up at Kipper.

'Good luck, Arthur,' Kipper whispered. 'And don't worry—I'm sure Tom will think of a way for us to help you.' Arthur smiled gratefully, then ran across to the open door of the Cheese Hall. He looked into the doorway and down the passage. No one was there, but he could hear footsteps.

Tom jumped as high as he could and bit one of the 'legs'.

He ran straight through the door. Snatcher was turning into the passage. Looking around desperately, Arthur's eye fell on a very large grandfather clock, just inside the door. Arthur opened its case, jumped inside, and pulled the door to. As he pushed against the pendulum and chains, the clock made a loud clang. Snatcher stopped in front of the clock.

'That's odd. It ain't been working for years.' He gave the clock a blow with his hornswoggle, made his way through the front door, and slammed it shut.

A very large grandfather clock

The Entrance Hall

He looked about

Chapter 3

INSIDE THE CHEESE HALL

In the passage all was quiet. Then the clock started striking, and as it did, there was also a fair bit of muffled squeaking. The chimes died away and the case slowly opened. A very startled Arthur stepped out. He shook his head and blinked, then crept along to the end of the passage. Through an archway was a large entrance hall.

Arthur listened. All was silent and the place was deserted. It seemed all the Members had gone out hunting, and he would have the Cheese Hall to himself for a while. But perhaps some of them had stayed behind—he would have to be as careful as he knew how.

He looked about. There was a large marble staircase, several doors, and high up on the walls ran a painted frieze. He studied the frieze in silence. It depicted the cheeses of the world—English cheeses frolicked in the fields, cave-bound French cheeses huddled in green and blue mounds, Swiss cheeses rolled down mountainsides, Norwegian cheeses leaped from cliffs into fjords, and some Welsh cheeses huddled under a bush in the rain. There were a number of other scenes, but Arthur couldn't work out what countries and cheeses they depicted. He wondered particularly about some small tins being carried by an elephant.

Some small tins being carried by an elephant

Above the frieze were statues set in alcoves. These he took to be of heroes of the cheese world. Most of them looked very miserable, apart from one who was clutching a flaming cheese aloft. This statue of a man had a mad grin on his face. Arthur walked over to a sign on the wall below this statue and read:

Malcolm of Barnsley
1618–1649
'He lives who has seen cheese combust by its own will'
Donated by the
Lactose Paranormal Research Council

Malcolm of Barnsley

Arthur wondered what this meant. Looking around he noticed that the doors all had small plaques fixed to them. He walked to the closest door and read:

The Members' Tea and Cake Room.

Ladies' Night—February 29th 5.30–6.00p.m.

Non-members keep out!

Arthur was not sure what he was looking for so he decided to read the plaques on all the other doors as well. On the second it read—

The Chairman's Suite

Entrance by invitation only

At the third . . .

Laboratory

And at the last . . .

KEEP OUT!

I wonder? Arthur thought, and he reached for the handle, turned it, and pushed. The door creaked open to reveal a long torch-lit passageway. Arthur listened to see if he could hear anybody. From further down he could just make out a soft bubbling sound. He listened for a minute or two, and then his curiosity got the better of him. He made his way quietly down the passage.

Reaching the end of the passage, he stopped. Before him was a large hexagonal stone chamber, with an open shaft in the centre of the floor. As he stood gazing about in wonderment he noticed a large yellow banner hanging from the balcony. In the centre of the banner was a picture of a wedge of cheese, and beneath it ran the words 'R.C.G. We Shall Rise Again!' His eyes moved to the open shaft in the centre of the floor, and he realized that this was the source of the bubbling sound. He walked forward, and then recoiled. The smell of cheese was overpowering. Holding his nose and keeping a little back from the edge of the hole, he looked down. The shaft descended into total darkness, and the bubbling was coming from somewhere below.

He moved back from the hole and looked about. 'I wonder where Fish and the others are?'

Arthur noticed a small wooden door on one side of the chamber, with a sign above it that read 'Members' Changing Room'. He quietly tried the door. It was locked.

'Bother!' he muttered under his breath. 'I'll have to go back to the hall and try the other doors.'

Arthur made his way back up the passageway to the entrance hall doorway, and listened carefully. All he could hear was the bubbling behind him, so he crept out into the entrance hall and looked at the three remaining doors.

'I don't think they would keep them in a tearoom, or the chairman's suite . . . so that leaves the lab.' He tried the lab door. It opened.

Arthur found himself at the top of a flight of steps that led down into a vast hall, filled with enormous silent machines

Arthur found himself at the top of a flight of steps that led down into a vast hall, filled with enormous silent machines. Stained-glass windows high in the walls cast an eerie light over everything. Arthur looked about then listened. He could hear nothing. He decided to risk making a noise.

'Fish . . . Fish . . . are you in here?' he whispered loudly. His voice reverberated alarmingly around the hall before it died away. There was no reply.

As his eyes became accustomed to the gloom, he noticed a pale red glow in a far corner of the lab. Arthur strained his eyes. It was an illuminated sign above some door or passage. It was too far away to read.

Arthur nervously made his way down the steps, and crept along the marble pathways between the silent machinery. The smell of oil and polished brass filled the air. Arthur studied the various machines and apparatus as he passed them by. He recognized some of the machines from his grandfather's bedroom, but his grandfather's were like toys by comparison. There was a beam engine even larger than the one on the laundry, lathes and enormous drills, milling machines, rows of glass tanks filled with liquid that had metal plates hung in them, a cart with an enormous coil of metal sitting on it, and something very large with canvas sheeting tied over it.

Finally he neared the glowing sign. It hung above an archway. Through the archway was a spiral staircase, that descended to somewhere below. He looked up and read—

DUNGEON

Arthur looked back around the hall, listened for a moment, and then braced himself. It looked very dark down those steps and Arthur felt nervous about what he might find there. He swallowed and started down.

He swallowed and started down

The dungeon

Arthur reached the bottom step

Chapter 4

THE DUNGEON

Arthur reached the bottom step, and stopped. Before him was a corridor with three cells on either side. The fronts of five of them were made from iron bars, and each had a door set into the bars. But the last cell on the right-hand side was boarded up. Arthur turned to the first cell and peered inside. Eyes stared back at him from the gloom. He could just make out the shapes of the creatures as they quivered against the back wall.

'Oh, poor things! They're underlings!' he said under his breath.

There was a boxtroll, three cabbageheads, and a rare two-legged lonely stoat. Arthur did not recognize any of them as his friends. He tried the lock, but it was no use.

'Don't worry,' he whispered through the bars. 'I'm a

There was a boxtroll, three cabbageheads, and a rare two-legged lonely stoat

friend. I'll get you out of here if I can!' Then he turned round and peered into the cell opposite. There was just a stack of small cardboard boxes, so he walked on. As he reached the next cell, there was a flash of movement from the darkness, and suddenly snarling heads appeared between the bars and snapped at him. Arthur jumped back. They were trotting badgers.

Suddenly snarling heads appeared between the bars and snapped at him

Arthur watched them till they stopped snapping, quietened down, and finally returned to the gloom at the back of their cell. Then, shakily, he turned to inspect the cell behind him. There were three more boxtrolls. For a moment Arthur felt his heart jump, but as soon as he took a better look he realized none of them were his friends. Again he tried the lock to no avail, and again he whispered some words of reassurance before moving on to investigate the last open cell.

Three very familiar cardboard boxes were stacked on top of each other. As soon as Arthur saw what was there he stopped and called out.

Three very familiar cardboard boxes were stacked on top of each other

'Fish! Shoe! Egg!' Arthur waited for a few moments, then eventually a head slowly rose from a hole in the top box. It was Fish.

Fish gave a loud gurgle, and heads, arms, and legs sprouted from all three boxes simultaneously. The stack fell

over with a clatter and was followed by a lot of moaning.
Titus was standing behind where the stack had once stood.
He smiled at Arthur. Arthur clutched the bars as his friends
rushed forward to meet him.

Arthur clutched the bars as his friends rushed forward to meet him

'Thank God you are all right!' exclaimed Arthur. 'We
have been so worried about you.'

Fish, Shoe, and Egg all gurgled excitedly, while Titus
squeaked. They all reached their hands through the bars
towards Arthur, and looked at him very hopefully.

'I am going to get you out of here!' Arthur said firmly.
'I promise.' He looked down at the lock. Fish followed his
glance.

'I don't suppose you know where the key is, do you?'
asked Arthur.

The underlings shook their heads and looked
disappointed. Arthur turned round. There was no key visible
anywhere, but his eye fixed on the boarded-up cell opposite.

It might be worth taking a look at that.

The underlings suddenly looked very nervous. Arthur took a step towards the boarded-up cell, but was stopped dead in his tracks. Several pairs of hands were gripping his clothes and holding him back.

'All right,' said Arthur. 'I won't go near it.'

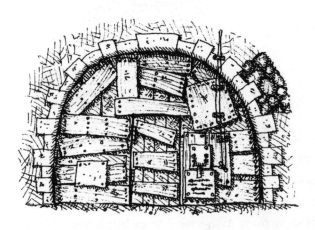

His eye fixed on the boarded-up cell

The hands holding his clothes let go. Arthur studied the front of the boarded-up cell. A large switch was fixed to the planks by its door, and underneath it, written in red paint, was—

> **Beware!**
> **Dangerous Prisoner!**
> **Put switch in upright position**
> **BEFORE entering the cell!**

'There must be something in there even worse than trotting badgers.' He turned back to the underlings. They were nodding their heads vigorously in agreement. 'What is it?' Arthur asked.

The underlings started jumping up and down, and making noises. 'Bonk! Bonk! Bonk!'

When they realized that Arthur had no idea what they meant, they gave up.

The underlings started jumping up and down,
and making noises. 'Bonk! Bonk! Bonk!'

'Well, I think I will leave it for the moment . . . I had better concentrate on getting you out of here!' The underlings looked relieved.

'I think the key must be upstairs somewhere. I'll go and see if I can find it. I will be back soon—I promise!' The boxtrolls and Titus huddled together in the cell and looked at Arthur with pleading eyes. It felt wrong to leave them alone again, but the only way he could help them was by finding the key to their cell, and his best chance of doing that was before the Members returned from the hunt.

Tearing his eyes away from them, Arthur turned and made for the steps, keeping well away from the boarded-up cell and the trotting badgers.

Arthur by the huge doors in the floor

Where would they keep the key?

Chapter 5

BACK IN THE LAB

Arthur crept up the stairs from the dungeon, and as he reached the top he checked again that no one was there.

Where would they keep the key? Arthur thought, and he started to search the lab. As he tiptoed amongst the machines he noticed some chains stretching down from the darkness to somewhere near the centre of the lab. After a while Arthur emerged from between machines, and found he was standing on a pathway that surrounded a large open area. Beyond waist-height railings were a huge set of iron doors, set in the floor. The chains that he'd seen were fixed to iron rings in the centre of the doors. High above hung a strange giant metal funnel. Its mouth pointed down towards the doors.

Arthur walked around the pathway. When he reached the far side there was a box fixed to the railings. Arthur looked at it. It was some kind of control panel. A metal tube ran down from beneath it, and through a small hole by the edge of the pathway. He peered down the hole. It was dark and very narrow, but he could just make out a pale light from somewhere deep below. Again he caught the strong smell of cheese.

There was a box fixed to the railings

I wonder what's down there? he said to himself.

He turned back to the control panel. There was an array of dials, and below them was a brass disc with a slot for a key in it. The slot was pointing to the word 'DOWN' that had been etched into the front panel. Across the panel was etched the word 'UP'. Arthur looked out across the doors, and then his eye followed the chains up towards the funnel. From the top of the funnel giant curling wires descended to the roof of what looked like an iron garden shed on stilts. This shed stood by the pathway, and overlooked the doors in the floor. Another pair of curly wires emerged from the shed roof, and led to a smaller funnel. This was fixed above the roof of a cage that stood on the floor of the lab next to the shed. Arthur looked into the empty cage. He had a bad feeling about it.

He had a bad feeling about it

There were steps leading up to a gantry that ran around the shed. Arthur was curious and made his way up them, then looked into the shed through its thick glass windows. A chair stood in front of a large console covered in buttons, levers, and switches. Behind the chair was a workbench covered in bits and pieces. There was some small machine with two funnels attached to it, some tools, a pile of cogs and springs . . . a wooden box . . . and . . . his wings.

Arthur rushed around to the door, and tried the handle. It was locked, so he went around to the back of the shed to get a better look. Yes! They were definitely his wings. And the wing spars and leatherwork had been mended. Then his heart stopped. They had taken the box to pieces!

He went around to the back of the shed to get a better look

'Oh no! What am I going to do now?' he muttered.

Arthur looked down at the floor of the lab. On a trolley close by were some tools. He rushed down and picked out a large hammer. With difficulty he lifted it, and returned to the shed. Arthur raised the hammer above his head and swung it at the window in the door.

The sound reverberated around the lab . . . and the hammer just bounced off the window! Arthur was startled. He crouched down and waited to see if the noise would bring anyone rushing in. The sound died away and nobody came. Arthur decided to try again. But again the hammer just bounced off.

'Darn it!' he muttered. 'I need to find keys!' Perhaps the keys for the shed and the keys for the cells would all be kept together somewhere.

*Arthur raised the hammer above his head
and swung it at the window in the door*

He looked about the lab. There didn't seem to be anywhere obvious that keys would be kept. Arthur climbed back down the steps, and placed the hammer back on the trolley. Then he made his way across the lab, and up the steps to the entrance hall.

For a few moments he waited to see if he could hear anybody, then crept across the entrance hall to the Chairman's Suite. It wasn't locked, and in a moment he was inside with the door closed.

The room was very dark, the only light coming from embers in a large fireplace. Arthur could just see the silhouette of a desk across the room. Carefully feeling his way, he crossed to the desk, and picked up an oil lamp which was sitting on it. Moving carefully over to the fireplace, he took a spill from the fire and lit the lamp. Suddenly Arthur felt very uneasy. The faces of generations of Snatchers stared down at him from family portraits on the walls.

Don't look at them, and you will feel better, Arthur told himself.

He turned his attention to the rest of the room. The desk was huge and very cluttered, and behind it heavy, moth-eaten velvet drapes covered the wall. In front of the fireplace were two decrepit sofas and a chaise longue. One of the sofas had an old blanket and a dirty sheet strewn over it, and next to it was a pile of dirty socks. The other sofa was a mess of horsehair and springs. Someone had cut its cloth covering away. The whole room smelt rather unpleasant.

Don't look at them, and you will feel better, Arthur told himself

The desk seemed the obvious place to look, so he walked over to it, and placed the lamp back down. He noticed an area in the centre of the desk had been cleared so a large sheet of paper could be laid out. This was held down at its corners by a paperweight, a dirty cup and saucer, and a pair of old boots. Arthur studied the sheet. It seemed to be some sort of scientific diagram, but more than that he could not tell.

Around it on the desk were stubs of old pencil, rubber bands, a broken pocket watch, the dried remains of half a sandwich, a ruler, and a broken quill . . . but no keys. Arthur decided to try the drawers. He walked around the desk and pulled open the first one.

Socks? Arthur was very surprised. The drawer was filled with socks, only a little less grubby than the pile by the sofa. Reluctantly he put his hand in and searched to see if there were any keys hidden there. When he decided there were not, he moved on.

Arthur opened the next drawer, and to his disgust he discovered it contained long johns. There was no way he was putting his hand in there. He took the ruler from the desk and used it to empty the drawer. Again there were no keys, so he put the underwear back, again using the ruler. Then he closed the drawer very firmly, dropped the ruler as hastily as he could, and shivered.

With a slight feeling of dread, he opened the next drawer. In this one he found a pink wig.

Arthur recognized it immediately—it was the wig Madame Froufrou had been wearing in the market. So there *was* a connection between her and Snatcher. But there was no time to think about that now—he had to concentrate on looking for the keys.

He lifted the wig out of the drawer, gave it a shake, and then hunted around the empty drawer. No keys!

Arthur replaced the wig, and moved on to the last drawer. This one was so full that it was hard to open, and he had to pull with all his might. When it finally sprang open, he found a great bundle of fabric crammed inside. He pulled it out and opened it up, then gave another gasp of recognition. It was Madame Froufrou's dress.

It was Madame Froufrou's dress

Things get curiouser and curiouser, Arthur thought. Then he checked the drawer for keys, and stuffed the dress back into it. It was not easy and took a certain amount of standing on to make it go back in.

Where next, Arthur wondered.

Looking about the room, he noticed a small table by one wall. There was a glass bottle on the table with some objects in it. Arthur walked over to the table and picked up the bottle. In the bottom, amongst some straw, was a tiny piece of cheese and two very small sleeping mice . . . or very, very, very, small rats.

In the bottom, amongst some straw, was a tiny piece of cheese and two very small sleeping mice . . . or very, very, very, small rats

As he stood looking at the tiny creatures in puzzlement, a sudden noise came from outside the room. It was footsteps—and they were approaching the door. Arthur froze for a second, then ran to the drapes and flung himself desperately behind them. A moment later someone entered the room. They made their way to the desk, and sat down in the chair behind it.

'My poor feet! This blooming rain!' It was Snatcher's voice.

Arthur peeped out from behind the curtains. Snatcher had his feet up on his desk and was unlacing his wet boots. Arthur watched as Snatcher took them off and swapped them with the dry pair on the desk. Then Snatcher stood up and walked over to the fireplace. He stood by the fire and pulled back his coat. Then Arthur saw them!

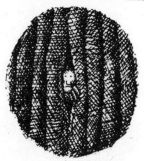

Arthur peeped out from behind the curtains

Hanging from a short piece of string attached to Snatcher's waistcoat was a large bunch of keys. After a few moments trying to warm himself, Snatcher gave up, turned, and walked out of the door, leaving it slightly ajar.

Hanging from a short piece of string attached to Snatcher's waistcoat was a large bunch of keys

Arthur crept out from behind the drapes and made his way across the room. He looked out into the hall and saw Snatcher standing in the archway facing the front door.

I have got to get those keys, thought Arthur. But how to do it—that was looking almost impossible. Then he heard a commotion from the passage.

He crept out of Snatcher's suite and made his way to the staircase

'Come on, me lads! How many cheeses did we get in the end?' Snatcher asked someone in the passage.

'Eight, I think!' came the reply.

With a sinking heart, Arthur realized that the hunt was returning, and that he needed to find a good hiding place—and quickly.

'Put the mutts in my suite,' Snatcher ordered.

Arthur looked back at the velvet drapes and thought better of it. It didn't seem a safe enough place. Then he looked at the staircase. Perhaps he could hide upstairs? He crept out of Snatcher's suite, made his way to the staircase, and started to climb as fast as he could. Behind him he heard more voices.

At the far end of the loft a pair of doors were open to the night sky

'The others made me be legs for the whole hunt!' It was Gristle.

'Stop your complaining, and get upstairs and man the cheese hoist,' Snatcher barked.

Arthur broke out into a cold sweat, and increased his pace up the stairs. As he reached the top he looked back. Gristle was just reaching the first step. Arthur rushed for the only door on the landing. In a second he was through it with the door closed.

He found himself in the roof space below the dome. Fenced pens filled with hay covered most of the floor. At the

far end of the loft a pair of doors were open to the night sky—these must be the doors that Bert had described.

He heard Gristle again. 'Oi! Master. Can you send me up some help? I'm knackered.'

Arthur felt sick. He rushed to the open doors and looked down. Far below in the street he could see huntsmen and cheese-hounds milling about.

'Oi! Snatcher! I can't lift these cheeses on me own!'

The shouting was getting closer. Arthur looked up. Above his head was a metal beam that protruded out above the street. A pulley with a rope going through it hung from the end of the beam.

The door behind him opened. Arthur held his breath and jumped for the rope.

The Cheese Hall
Dome &
Attic
1/120 SCALE

Cross section of the Cheese Hall roof and dome

Arthur sat on the bridge of the roof and recovered his breath

Chapter 6

OUT ON THE ROOF!

He had only just made it. Arthur sat on the bridge of the roof and recovered his breath. It was still raining, and a few inches behind him was a vertical drop to the street. He did not feel happy.

Keeping his eyes straight ahead, Arthur shuffled along the roof until he reached the statues below the dome. From inside the roof he could hear muffled voices.

Then a metallic squeaking started. Arthur looked round. He could just see the pulley at the end of the metal beam. The wheel in the pulley was turning and a rope was slowly passing through it. Whatever it was lifting, it was heavy.

The plaintive bleating of cheeses grew louder.

'The poor things,' Arthur muttered, then he looked up at the dome. If he could get up there he might be able to signal to the laundry.

Without his wings he would have to climb. This made him feel very nervous. It felt so different not being able to fly. Holding on to a statue Arthur stood up slowly and started to climb. He made his way up the stonework and onto the dome. There were a few tiles missing and he found that he could use the battens beneath as steps. Soon he was hanging onto the weathervane on the plinth.

He made his way up the stonework and onto the dome

Looking across the town he could just make out the mast of the Nautical Laundry. Black specks floated around it. Arthur guessed it must be the crows. He waved but he was pretty sure they wouldn't see him. The rain grew heavier, and soon he lost sight of the crows. He looked down. Set into the dome were several small round windows. These, he thought, must act as lights for the loft. He decided to have a look and see what was going on in there.

Arthur turned round slowly, lowered himself till he found a footing, and then released his grip on the weathervane. He made his way down to a narrow strip of stonework that ran around the base of the dome. One of the windows was just a few feet from him. He eased himself along the ledge and peered in. Below he could see that the pens were now occupied by cheeses. He moved around to the far window so he could see what was happening by the hoist.

Several men were pulling something up. After a great deal of rope had been pulled in, a net came into view. More cheeses! Arthur could hear the bleating. When the net was level with the doors, one of the Members took a long pole with a hook on the end, and used it to pull the net into the loft. Then the doors were shut and the cheeses released from the net. For about a minute there was mayhem as the cheeses did all they could to evade capture. But trapped in the loft the cheeses stood no chance, and soon they were all in pens.

Several men were pulling something up

The cheeses quietened down, and the Members disappeared downstairs. Arthur decided it was too dangerous to try and get back down the hoist and, besides,

Arthur peered through it

the loft doors were shut. But he had to get back in somehow. He looked at the little window in front of him and decided to try to force it open. It gave way fairly easily, and swung open without too much noise. Arthur peered through it. Directly below him was a pen, with a good covering of hay on the floor, which Arthur thought might make a soft landing. He turned around, lowered himself through the window, and dropped. He hit the floor, just avoiding a cheese, and fell back into the hay. The cheeses in the pen started bleating noisily. Arthur sat still, hoping their noise would not bring any of the huntsmen back. But as the bleating died down he heard footsteps coming up the stairs. He groaned inwardly, but quickly covered himself in the hay and lay very still. Then he heard the door.

'Them cheeses is making a right commotion! You'd think they knew what was going to happen to them!' said a voice. It was Gristle. 'Let the cage down, and get them out the pens. Snatcher says that the Great One is going to be right hungry after they give him a good zap!'

Arthur sat still and waited for the bleating to stop

'What they going to use tonight?' asked another voice.

'Those awful trotting badgers. The sooner we cut them down to size the better!' replied Gristle. 'Did you see what they did to the Trouts?'

'Yes. Old Trout won't be able to sit down any time soon, and Trout Junior is lucky he still has a nose.'

'I am blooming glad it ain't us on lab duty tonight,' muttered Gristle. 'Anyway, they'll be done in there in about ten minutes, and so we better get on.'

Arthur peered out through the hay and saw Gristle and two other men were now standing in the loft. Gristle was standing by a pair of brass levers that stuck out of the wall.

'Move yerselves then,' ordered Gristle. 'Don't want to squash yer.'

The other men cleared a space under the centre of the dome, and Gristle pushed one of the levers down. Arthur followed the men's gaze upwards. A cage was descending from inside the very top of the dome. It clanked and shook as it moved slowly towards the floor of the loft. The cheeses were silent. The cage settled on the floor and came to rest.

'Right!' said Gristle. 'Get the cage door open, and let's get the cheeses in.'

While one of the men held the door open, Gristle and the other man grabbed cheeses from the pens and pushed them into the cage. Soon the cage was full.

Gristle and the other man grabbed cheeses and pushed them into the cage

'I do hope the Great One is hungry! Eight is an awful lot of cheese,' said the doorman.

'Don't worry, he is getting really BIG!' smirked Gristle. 'Snatcher says he will be ready real soon. All we have to do is keep up the supply of cheese and monsters.'

Arthur felt cold when he heard this. What was going on?

'Oi! Gristle! D'yer think they're ready yet?'

'The music ain't started! They 'ave to 'ave the music before the cheese goes in the pit. Otherwise it wouldn't be a Cheese Ceremony . . . would it?' Gristle replied. 'Just keep your ear out for the din.'

All was silent in the cheese loft until strange music started to waft up from somewhere below. Arthur had never heard anything like it before. It was a crazed drumming and blowing of horns. It reached a crescendo then stopped.

Gristle raised a hand then whispered, ''Ere we go!' He

pushed down the second lever. There was a loud bang and a trapdoor beneath the cage opened. The cage full of cheeses shuddered. Gristle pushed the first lever down and the cage started to disappear down through the hole.

After about thirty seconds Gristle spoke again. 'Look! The chain's gone floppy. It must have hit the fondue!'

'Let it sink slowly, then after about a minute haul it up,' whispered one of the others. 'Don't want no half-cooked cheeses hanging about!'

Arthur watched the men in silence. After a minute or so Gristle brought the cage back up. It came back through the floor . . . empty. From the bottom of the cage hung a few strings of molten cheese. Arthur felt horrified. Gristle stopped the cage, then snapped the trapdoor lever up, and the door in the floor closed.

'Done!' said Gristle. 'Now time for tea and biscuits.'

The Members trooped out of the loft and closed the door. Arthur had witnessed something awful, but he was not sure quite what.

From the bottom of the cage hung a few strings of molten cheese

Kipper suddenly burst through the door with Tom on his platform

Mildred telling her news to Willbury, Marjorie, and the captain

Chapter 7

BACK AT THE SHIP

In the captain's cabin Mildred had finished telling her news to Willbury, Marjorie, and the captain, and they were all waiting rather anxiously over cups of cocoa, when Kipper suddenly burst through the door with Tom on his platform.

'He's inside!' said Kipper.

Willbury looked at Tom and Kipper. Then his face fell. 'Where's Arthur?'

'He's INSIDE!' repeated Kipper.

'Not the Cheese Hall?' said Willbury. He was met with silence. 'I don't believe it. How come Arthur is inside the Cheese Hall, and you're here? You're supposed to be looking after him.'

Tom looked rather guilty. 'After Mildred left, we started to follow them, but Snatcher came back. So we hid in the alley, and Snatcher left the door open while he went to get something . . . and Arthur says to me to distract Snatcher's horse . . . and he would sneak in . . . ' Tom paused, and looked even guiltier. 'So I did . . . '

Willbury closed his eyes and shook his head.

The captain looked very stern and took over the questioning. 'What happened then?'

The captain looked very stern and took over the questioning

Tom and Kipper both looked very upset. Kipper looked at the floor and started to speak. 'Well, Arthur rushes in, and a few moments later Snatcher comes out and locks the door. Then he gets on his horse and rides off . . . '

Tom followed on. 'So I says to Kipper that we better wait for Arthur to come out again. So we wait in the alley . . . for about an hour or so . . . ' his voice trailed off.

'Yes . . . ' said the captain.

' . . . then the hunt came back . . . ' Tom's voice quavered.

'Do you mean Arthur's trapped inside there, with Snatcher and his mob?' asked Willbury.

' Yes . . . ' Now Tom was looking at the floor too.

'What on earth do I do now?' Willbury muttered to himself. 'I am not sure he'll be able to get out of the Cheese Hall. Even if he doesn't get caught I think he's trapped.'

'It's a pity he hasn't got his wings,' added the captain. 'He might have been able to get away if he had those.'

There was a knocking from outside. The captain opened the window and two crows hopped in.

''Scuse us, captain!' said the crows. 'But we just saw something over at the Cheese Hall.' Everybody turned to look at the crows. 'We think we just saw Arthur on the roof. He's not there now but we're pretty sure it was him.'

'Can you go over there right away and see if you can find him?' asked Willbury.

'Surely,' said the crows. 'We'll go right now.'

With that the crows hopped out of the window, and flew off.

With that the crows hopped out of the window, and flew off

Inside the tearoom

He could hear distant laughing, and the chinking of crockery

Chapter 8

Tea and Cake

Arthur climbed out of the pen, crept across to the door at the top of the stairs, and opened it a few inches. He could hear distant laughing, and the chinking of crockery. He closed the door again.

What am I going to do, he wondered. If he went down now, he was sure to get caught.

He turned and looked at the cage that stood in the centre of the floor. It was a very sad sight. Arthur climbed back into one of the pens and lay down in the hay to think.

'I've got to get back downstairs to rescue the underlings . . . and what am I going to do about my wings? I'll never be able to put them back together without Grandfather . . . ' Arthur sat up and pulled out his doll. 'Grandfather! I've forgotten about Grandfather.'

Arthur sat up and pulled out his doll

He wound the doll, and then called his grandfather's name. He heard his voice reply.

'Arthur! Where have you been? Where are you? Are you all right?'

'I am all right, Grandfather . . . but I am in the loft above the Cheese Hall.'

'WHAT? You're in the Cheese Hall?' Grandfather sounded angry.

'Yes . . . ' said Arthur, then he explained what had happened.

'Oh, Arthur! Why can't you do what you're told? I'm very cross with you . . . and Mr Nibble. He should never have let you get into this trouble.'

'It's not his fault. He told me not to take any chances and I disobeyed him . . . and you.'

'Well, we will talk about this later!' Grandfather sounded very serious. 'But for now, we'll have to get you out of there. You say you have seen your wings?'

'Oh, Arthur! Why can't you do what you're told?'

'Yes, the spars and leatherwork have been mended, but all the workings in the box have been taken to pieces.'

'That's not a problem. If you can find a few tools I can tell you how to put them back together, if you can just find a way of getting your hands on them,' Grandfather said. 'Then you'll be able to escape!'

'If you can find a few tools I can tell you how to put them back together'

Arthur paused before he spoke again. 'I have to help the underlings escape as well.'

'Yes,' said Grandfather, 'but you'll be no use to them if you can't escape yourself. You need to get your wings fixed.'

'It might be tricky with Snatcher and the Members around . . . '

'Maybe, but everybody has to sleep.'

'What do you think they are up to?' asked Arthur.

'I am not sure . . . But I am pretty sure it's no good!' Grandfather sounded worried. 'Something strange is going on. This Great One that needs cheese . . . and they said they needed more "monsters" as they call the poor underlings . . . And those things you saw in the lab. It's all very peculiar.'

'What should I do now?' asked Arthur.

'If you hide for a while, I bet the Members will go to sleep before too long. Then get down to the lab and find a way of getting the wings. I'll guide you through rebuilding the motor.'

'All right, Grandfather. And how are you doing?'

'This damp is getting worse and all my joints are aching. About an hour ago I heard some rumbling. It sounds as if some of the caves are starting to crumble. I don't know what those damn boxtrolls think they are playing at. They are supposed to keep this place dry, and shored up.'

Arthur felt worried about Grandfather. 'Are you going to be all right?'

'I'll be fine. Anyway, you get some rest! Contact me as soon as you get hold of your wings.'

'I will, Grandfather . . . and keep warm!'

The crackling from the doll stopped and Arthur lay back in the hay. He tried to concentrate on the noise from downstairs, but soon his eyes closed and he dropped off to sleep.

He awoke with a start. Something long and yellow was pecking his nose. He sat up, and as he did two black shapes flapped up and settled on the edge of the pen.

'Sorry if we startled you.' It was a pair of crows.

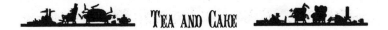

'You did!' replied Arthur as he rubbed his nose. 'But I'm pleased to see you!' The crows must have flown in through the window he'd forced open.

Something long and yellow was pecking his nose

'We're from the laundry. The captain and the others are very worried about you.'

'How did you know I was here?' Arthur asked.

'We saw you on top of the dome earlier, and we reported it to the captain, and your friends. They asked us to fly over here to see if we could find you.'

'Thanks,' said Arthur. 'Can you take a message back to them for me?'

'No problem!' cawed one of the crows.

'Tell them that I've found the underlings in the dungeon under this place . . . and Snatcher and the Members have built some huge weird device . . . And they are doing really nasty things to cheeses . . . Oh! And I have found out where my wings are . . . '

'You've been busy then. Is there anything else we can do?' asked the other crow.

Arthur thought for a moment, and then listened. There was no noise from downstairs. 'Yes. Do you think you could fly down the outside of the building and check through the windows to see if Snatcher and his mob are asleep?'

'No sooner said than done! It won't take a jiffy.' The crows set off through the open window in the dome and disappeared. After about a minute they returned.

'It's all clear. We flew round the whole building and looked in every window we could. They're all asleep in a big room at the front. Looks like they've had a right feast of cake. Even that Snatcher is in there, snoring away.'

'We flew round the whole building and looked in every window'

'Good!' said Arthur. 'I'm going to try to free the underlings, and get my wings back.'

'Anything else?' asked the crows.

'No. Just tell them what I've told you . . . ' Arthur paused, ' . . . and tell them we'll all be back soon.'

The crows disappeared and Arthur set off down the stairs.

When he reached the bottom he crept across to the tearoom. As quietly as he could he opened the door. About thirty men were strewn across sofas and old armchairs, and were surrounded by the debris of an enormous feast of tea and cake. On the far side of the room in the largest armchair was slumped the sleeping Snatcher.

About thirty men were strewn across sofas and old armchairs

A cold sweat broke out on Arthur's forehead. He would have to be very, very careful. Trying not to make the slightest noise he made his way into the room and started to weave his way between the furniture, towards Snatcher. With each step he tried to avoid the abandoned teacups and plates on the floor. Slowly he got closer. The legs of one of the Members lay across his path and Arthur stepped over them. As he did the hem of his vest brushed the Member's foot.

'CAKE!'

Arthur jumped forward and turned. It was Gristle.

The hem of his vest brushed the Member's foot

'. . . just one more slice . . . I love cake . . . ' Gristle's eyes
were still closed. He was talking in his sleep. Arthur closed
his eyes for a moment and swallowed. He checked about the
room and saw that nobody else was stirring, then made the
last few steps to Snatcher.

The keyring hung on a string from Snatcher's waistcoat.
There was a gentle jingling as Snatcher's enormous belly
moved in and out.

Amongst a few crumbs on a cake stand that stood on the
floor in front of Snatcher was a knife. Arthur picked it up,
and gently took hold of the keys. He held the knife to the
string and as Snatcher's belly moved the knife cut slowly
into the string. The string separated and for a moment
Snatcher's belly wobbled. Arthur held his breath. Snatcher
snorted . . . but didn't wake. Arthur put the knife down and
crept out of the room to the lab.

The knife cut slowly into the string

Once in the lab he decided that it would be better to get his wings before releasing the underlings. Grandfather was right—if he got caught himself, it would be all over. He just had to hope that Snatcher's keyring had all the keys he needed. Arthur rushed to the shed and made his way up the steps. Searching amongst the keys he found one that fitted the door. He slid it in the lock and turned. There was a satisfying clunk. He tried the handle, and the door opened. His wings were still on the bench. Arthur reached inside his suit and took out his doll.

'Grandfather! Are you there?'

'Yes, Arthur.'

'I am in the lab with the wings. Can you help me put them back together?'

'Certainly, Arthur. Can you find a small screwdriver and an adjustable spanner?'

Arthur looked about the bench and found the tools he needed. 'Yes! I've found them.'

'Good.'

Over the next hour Grandfather instructed as Arthur rebuilt the wings' motor. Occasionally Arthur looked up to check the door to the entrance hall, or would have to break

Over the next hour Grandfather instructed as Arthur rebuilt the wings' motor

off to wind up the doll when his grandfather's voice started to fade. Finally the motor was back together. Arthur smiled and thanked Grandfather.

'I think it would be a good idea if you put the wings on and wound them up . . . just in case,' said Grandfather.

'You're right,' replied Arthur as he strapped the wings on. 'I will speak to you later. I've got underlings to rescue before Snatcher wakes up!'

Arthur strapping the wings on

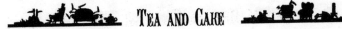 

'Very well, Arthur,' said Grandfather. 'But make sure you call me as soon as you are out of there! And please, please try not to take any unnecessary risks.'

Arthur put the doll away and wound up his wings. Then he locked the shed and made his way back downstairs. He peered in nervously at the Members, but they were all still snoring away. Arthur prayed that they would stay asleep for long enough. Tiptoeing on, he headed back towards the dungeon.

Arthur looked down the length of the dungeon

Fish shook his head and gave him a thumbs up

Chapter 9

AN ESCAPE?

Arthur looked down the length of the dungeon and stopped in his tracks. The door of the trotting badgers' cell stood open. He glanced across to his friends' cell. The four of them were still pressed up against the bars, obviously waiting for him to come back. They looked very happy to see him. He silently pointed to the open cell door. Fish shook his head and gave him a thumbs up.

Arthur still felt wary and mouthed the words, 'HAVE THEY GONE?'

Fish nodded his head. Arthur sighed with relief, and made his way to his friends' cell. As he passed the open door he remembered what the Members had said about them in the loft. Now the trotting badgers' cell looked very empty, and he felt an odd sensation of pity as he walked past it. Then he reached his friends' cell.

The underlings ran out and hugged him

'Thank God you are still here!' said Arthur.

The underlings looked happy.

'I am going to get you out of here,' Arthur said and produced the keys. He unlocked the door, and the underlings ran out and hugged him. Arthur hugged them back.

'Now,' said Arthur. 'We had better unlock the others.'

Fish pointed to the cells with the other underlings in, and nodded.

'What about the boarded-up cell?' The underlings looked across at it, and shook their heads.

'Why not?' asked Arthur.

Again they started to jump up and down, and quietly made bonk! bonk! noises.

'I'll trust your judgement,' Arthur said, feeling a little nervous. 'It might be very dangerous to release whatever is in there.' The underlings looked relieved.

Arthur unlocked the other underlings, and his friends went into the cells to reassure the other creatures that they could trust Arthur. Soon all of them stood at the bottom of the stairs.

Arthur checked that the coast was clear

'Come on!' said Arthur. 'We have to get out of here quickly . . . but remember to keep very quiet.' The underlings nodded and set off, following Arthur.

He guided the underlings up the stairs and out through the lab to the door to the entrance hall. They stopped and Arthur opened the door just enough to check that the coast was clear. Arthur was about to lead the underlings out into the entrance hall, when there was a loud cheese bleat from the passageway to the front door. Arthur and the underlings froze. After a few seconds the door of the tearoom opened and a sleepy Gristle walked out.

A voice followed him. 'It'll be the milkman. Tell 'im to leave fifteen pints and that I will pay 'im next week.' It was Snatcher . . .

Arthur watched as Gristle disappeared down the passage. Then he heard Gristle shout.

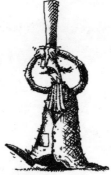

The door of the tearoom opened and a sleepy Gristle walked out

''Ave you got the keys to the front door?'

Arthur felt a lump in his throat. He looked from the archway to the passage across to the tearoom.

There was a pause then Snatcher's voice boomed from the tearoom. 'Someone's nicked me blooming keys!'

Arthur opened the door and ushered the underlings forward. 'Up the stairs! Run for your lives!' he whispered.

Just as they started to scuttle across the hall, there was a commotion from the tearoom and Snatcher stepped through the door. Arthur looked at Snatcher in horror. This might be the end of everything.

Arthur looked at Snatcher in horror

Unable to control the panic in his voice, Arthur turned to the underlings and shouted:

'RUN!'

The underlings rushed up the stairs. Arthur pushed the buttons on the front of the wing box and jumped. Thank goodness he could fly again.

'It's that blasted boy again. And he's stolen my wings!' shouted Snatcher. The other Members were now piling out into the entrance hall. They all looked up at Arthur, then at the underlings fleeing up the stairs.

'Get 'em!' screamed Snatcher as he pointed to the underlings. There was a coat stand that Arthur had not noticed before by the door of the tearoom. Snatcher grabbed a walking stick from it, and raised it to throw at the underlings. Arthur realized he still had the keys in his hand and threw them hard at Snatcher. They caught him in the face and Snatcher wailed at Arthur.

'You little swine. Just you wait till I get 'old of you!' But Arthur was already too far off the ground for Snatcher to reach.

They caught him in the face

The statue toppled over

Some of the Members had reached the stairs and were gaining on the underlings. Arthur adjusted his wing speed and flew up to one of the alcoves above the Members and grabbed hold of the statue. Then he pulled it hard. The statue toppled over. Below, the Members saw what was

The Members saw what was happening

happening and ran back down the stairs to get out of the way. The statue crashed down on the stairs.

Snatcher screamed again. 'Don't let 'im stop yer! Get those Monsters!' He grabbed another walking stick and waved it at the Members.

Arthur flew to the next statue and waited till some of the Members were brave enough to start mounting the stairs again, then he pulled on the second statue. Again there was a crash as the statue hit the stairs, and again the Members ran back to avoid it.

The underlings were just reaching the door to the loft. Arthur watched them rush through it and disappear. He came down on the landing, turned off his wings, ran through the door, and slammed it closed. As he did a walking stick clattered against the door behind him.

The underlings were standing in the loft looking scared out of their wits. Arthur looked around—they needed to barricade the door before the Members made it to the top of the stairs. His eyes fixed on the cage. He turned on his wings again, flew to the top of the cage, and unhooked it from its chain.

'Quick! Push this cage against the door,' Arthur shouted to the underlings.

The underlings obeyed and soon the cage crashed against the door. Arthur flew to the doors at the far end of the loft and pulled them open. The net was hanging from the end of the beam.

The cage crashed against the door

'Fish. Let out a bit of the rope so I can get the net into the loft!' Arthur ordered. Fish untied the rope and let a little play out. Arthur grabbed the net and pulled it back into the loft. He turned off his wings and spread the net out on the floor.

'Everybody but Fish get in the net.' The underlings looked horrified and didn't move.

'Quick!' shouted Arthur. There was a crashing as the Members threw themselves against the door. 'This is our only chance! Please get in the net.' Fish looked scared.

More crashing and shouting came from the stairway door. Reluctantly the underlings climbed into the net, and Arthur joined Fish at the rope.

As soon as the underlings were assembled in the centre of the net, Arthur and Fish pulled the rope in. There was a fearful squeaking and moaning, and the net swung out over the street.

'When you get to the ground, get out of the net and make for the canal,' Arthur called over to the underlings. He felt Fish nudge him. Fish was uncertain whether he was going to be left behind.

The net swung out over the street

'You and I are going to fly,' said Arthur.

Slowly they paid the rope out and the frightened creatures disappeared.

The crashing at the door grew louder, and Arthur and Fish let the rope out faster.

Finally the rope went limp.

'Right, Fish. Let's be off.' Fish backed away from Arthur as the cage behind them toppled over, crashing to the floor as the door flew open. Arthur grabbed Fish by the box corners and pushed him forward towards the drop to the street. As they reached the edge, he released Fish for a moment, turned the power knob on his box to full, hit both buttons, and then grabbed hold of Fish again.

For about two seconds they dropped

'Get them!' screamed a voice. The Members were racing across the loft. Arthur jumped and pushed Fish over the edge.

For about two seconds they dropped, then the wings started to beat and their descent slowed. Below them they could see the underlings running up a street in the direction of the canal, apart from the lonely stoat who was disappearing in the opposite direction looking miserable. From above screams of rage rang out.

'Stop them! Thieves! Kidnappers! Underlings! Monsters!' Then Arthur heard Snatcher's voice. 'Get downstairs and after them. They are not to get away!'

Arthur spoke to Fish. 'Fish, do you want me to put you down?'

Fish turned his head and shook it. Arthur could see that Fish was smiling.

'So you enjoy flying?'

Fish nodded, and started to gently flap his arms.

'Right then, I think we'd better catch up with the others.'

So they set off through the early morning light back to the laundry. After they had gone a few streets they heard the sound of dogs.

'They are coming after us!'

The lonely stoat disappeared in the opposite direction looking miserable

'Back to the laundry! Follow us.'

Arthur and Fish kept low as they flew

Chapter 10

ATTACK ON THE SHIP

Arthur and Fish kept low as they flew. They caught up with the underlings and Arthur shouted to them.

'Back to the laundry! Follow us.'

Arthur was surprised how fleet-footed the underlings were, but still the sound of the cheese-hounds grew louder. Soon they turned on to the canal bank and before them was the laundry. The rain had stopped and the washing was blowing in the wind. There was a shout from the deck followed by a commotion.

'Are you all right?' Arthur asked Fish. There was a happy gurgling.

The other underlings ran along the towpath and Arthur landed by the gangplank. As he landed he released Fish.

'Arthur! Fish! . . . Egg . . . Shoe . . . Titus . . . You got out!'

Arthur turned to see a very happy Willbury

Arthur turned to see a very happy Willbury standing at the top of the gangplank with Kipper, Tom, Marjorie, and the captain.

'Yes! We're all right!'

'Thank God, and well done!' Everyone looked delighted, and Kipper and Tom looked extremely relieved.

A shout came from somewhere on deck. 'Dogs ahoy!'

Arthur and Willbury turned to see the cheese-hounds rushing on to the towpath.

Arthur and Willbury turned to see the cheese-hounds rushing on to the towpath

'Quick, get the underlings aboard,' said Willbury. Fish, Shoe, Egg, and Titus led the underlings up the gangplank. The others seemed much more trusting now they could see that the four leaders knew Willbury as well as Arthur, and they followed without a murmur. Arthur ran on to the ship after them.

'Draw up the gangplank!' shouted the captain. Snatcher and his mob were now running down the towpath behind the dogs, roaring in anger. The crew hauled the gangplank up just before the first of the hounds leapt on to it.

'Load the cannon!'

'I told you, captain, we ain't got any gunpowder!'

'OK, OK! Prepare the knickers!' Crows flew down from the crow's-nest to the underwear section of the rigging, un-pegged six pairs of the largest knickers they could find, and then descended to the deck. The pirates quickly tied the knickers to various fixing points on the gunwales of the ship.

Crows with a particularly large pair of pants

From below decks came a scampering, and rats appeared carrying oddly shaped lumps, each the size of a tennis ball.

Rats appeared carrying oddly shaped lumps, each the size of a tennis ball

'What are those?' asked Arthur.

'We thought we might be attacked so Tom suggested that we make something to give the enemy a real surprise,' said the captain. 'We mixed all the gunge from the bilge pumps with glue, and then rolled it into balls. They were very sticky so we coated them in breadcrumbs and fluff. We tested one earlier . . . it's disgusting; if they hit you they burst and cover you in slime. It stinks and it is almost impossible to wash off.'

'Knickers loaded, Captain!' came the cry from the crew.

'Prepare to fire!' shouted the captain. The knickers were pulled back to form deadly catapults.

The knickers were pulled back to form deadly catapults

On the towpath everything went quiet, then a voice called out. It was Snatcher's.

'Board the laundry!'

As the cheese-hounds continued to jump up and down on the towpath, baying, the Members approached the ship. As they did the captain shouted:

'FIRE!'

'Fire!'

The twanging of six enormous pairs of knickers could be heard, followed by a whizzing, a splodging, and disgusted screams. The cheese-hounds ran back down the towpath to a safe distance. The Members looked as if they wanted to run too, but Snatcher was having none of it.

Snatcher was having none of it

'Go on, you weak-willed, yellow-bellied varmints! BOARD the laundry!' ordered Snatcher.

The captain shouted 'Fire!' again, and another volley flew over the side of the ship. More screams could be heard. This time one of the screams was Snatcher's.

'Retreat!' shouted Snatcher.

The Members didn't need telling twice. They ran back down the towpath to join the hounds, and the crew of the laundry cheered.

The Members didn't need telling twice

'I think we have got them on the run,' said the captain.

'They will think twice about attacking us again,' agreed Arthur.

'I hope you're right . . . ' said Willbury thoughtfully.

Along the towpath a meeting was being held. The group huddled around Snatcher, listening. Everybody on the Nautical Laundry watched. After a minute or so one of the Members ran off down the towpath and disappeared. Snatcher walked a little way back towards the ship, and shouted.

'You may have beaten us back, but it's not over yet!'

'Er hmm!' Arthur heard someone behind him and turned.

'Did you see Pickles and Levi?' It was the captain.

Arthur looked at the captain and could see he was waiting nervously for his reply.

'I am afraid I didn't,' said Arthur.

'No rodents at all?' asked the captain.

'Just a pair of tiny mice in Snatcher's room. And they were hardly big enough to be mice . . . '

The captain sighed, and turned away.

'Just a pair of tiny mice in Snatcher's room.'

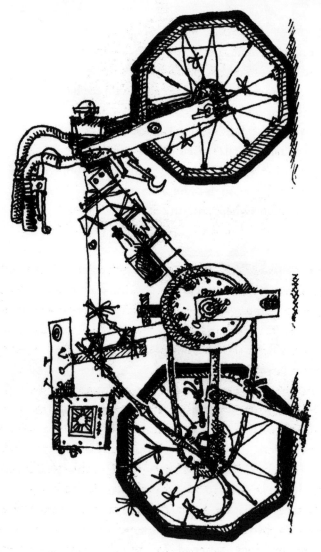

A Dodgy Tanner

The Ratbridge Irregular Police Force on 'Dodgy Tanners'

Chapter 11

THE POLICE

The bicycles that the Ratbridge Irregular Police Force rode were known as 'Dodgy Tanners'. This was because of the shape and number of their wheels. They had two wheels the shape of thrupenny bits. If one added together two thrupenny bits, one would have sixpence, and a sixpenny coin was known as a tanner.

Penny Farthing bicycles had perfectly round wheels like the coins they were named after. Thrupenny bits were many sided. Wheels this shape did not make for the good humour of the riders. On hard surfaces such as cobbles, the policemen could be heard a long way off, as they let out little cries of pain at every turn of the wheels. Many a burglar had made an early escape because of the warning noises of an unhappy approaching rider. Some policemen even took to wearing cushions strapped to their bottoms to prevent bruising. But not all could afford padding, so the Irregulars were known locally as 'Squeakers'.

Many a burglar had made an early escape because of the warning noises of an unhappy approaching rider

The Squeakers now came down the towpath as fast as they could without causing themselves too much discomfort. Emergency calls were rare, and as the Squeakers were paid by the number of incidents they attended, and arrests they made, they were in a rush to get to the scene. As they approached all fell silent.

The Chief Squeaker dismounted from his bike, unstrapped his cushion, and turned.

'Hello, hello, hello. What's going on here?'

The Chief Squeaker dismounted from his bike, and unstrapped his cushion

The Members and the pirates all looked very uneasy.

Snatcher made the first reply. 'We are being attacked by this bunch of cut-throats and robbers!'

'Attacked you say?' replied the officer.

'Yes! We were out for a peaceful stroll when these scallywags started firing at us. They need locking up!'

The sound of twenty pairs of iron handcuffs being prepared could be heard.

The sound of twenty pairs of iron handcuffs being prepared could be heard

'This sounds very serious!' replied the Chief Squeaker with a smile. 'It sounds as if a lot of arrests might need to be made!'

'That is balderdash!' called Willbury from the deck. 'We are just defending ourselves. I am a lawyer and . . . '

The Chief Squeaker raised his hand. 'A LAWYER!'

He went bright red. 'I don't think this is the sort of thing a lawyer should be mixed up in, but I expect no better. Officers, arrest that man!'

There was a rush for the ship.

'Stop!' cried Willbury. 'And a circuit judge!'

'WHOA!' cried the Chief Squeaker. 'I am very sorry, m'lud, I did not realize that you were so obviously honest. Men, arrest the party on the towpath.'

The policemen turned to the Members, still brandishing their handcuffs. But then Snatcher walked forward and spoke. 'The difference between me an 'im is CHALK and CHEESE.' Then he made a funny little sign with his hands.

Then he made a funny little sign with his hands

The police stopped in their tracks. The Chief Squeaker now spoke again in a quavering voice.

'Did you say CHALK and CHEESE?'

'Yes I did!' replied Snatcher.

'What kind of CHEESE is that?' As the Chief Squeaker spoke his hands made a number of strange gestures.

Snatcher replied, 'That would be a BIG CHEESE!' And he made the same gestures with his hands.

'Why is he doing that?' asked Arthur.

'I am not sure,' said a hesitant Willbury.

Marjorie sidled up to them. 'I think they are "Brothers"! Members of the Guilds.'

'What's that?' asked Arthur.

'Secret organizations. They are making secret signs to each other, and using code words to let each other know they are Members!'

'Why don't they just recognize each other?' Arthur asked.

'It's a very big organization, and there are lots of smaller parts of it. The police probably have their own section,' said Marjorie.

The policemen looked at each other and then fell to their knees. They then bowed their heads and whispered, 'We smell strong cheese! We smell strong cheese! It is overpowering. We respect it for it is the most flavoursome, and we are humble. What would it have us do?'

'We smell strong cheese! We smell strong cheese! It is overpowering.'

Snatcher smirked at the policemen fawning before him, then he spoke.

'I think you will find that "m'lud" might well be retired. He holds no power now—and he is harbouring a thief who has stolen a pair of mechanical wings from me. From me— A BIG CHEESE! I think that the right course of action would be to arrest the rapscallion who has stolen my wings and return them to me!'

The Chief Squeaker stood up, and turned to look at Willbury.

'Is this so, sir? You are no longer a judge?' he asked.

'Technically that is true . . . ' replied Willbury.

And before Willbury had a chance to go any further the Chief Squeaker cut in. 'Right! Drop your gangplank, sir! Any failure to do so will be seen as hindering the police in the course of their duties, and may force me to arrest you, and your entire crew.'

Willbury looked shocked. 'I think we'd better do what he says, otherwise we are going to get into real trouble.'

The pirates reluctantly lowered the gangplank.

As soon as it was lowered the Chief Squeaker shouted out, 'Arrest the boy!'

The policemen on the towpath rushed onto the ship. Kipper and the other pirates looked as if they were ready for a fight, and the policemen looked nervous.

'Hold back, crew!' said Willbury. Then he whispered to Arthur, 'Quick! Fly!'

But it was useless. Arthur had not thought to wind his wings up again, and they had no power left in them after the escape. The policemen grabbed him and snapped handcuffs around his wrists. He was then marched off the ship and the Chief Squeaker removed his wings.

The policemen grabbed him, and snapped handcuffs around his wrists

Arthur's heart sank. He thought he'd done so well to get himself and the underlings safely out of the Cheese Hall— he couldn't believe this was happening to him now. Just when he'd got his wings back, to have them taken away from him again! And for the police to be on Snatcher's side! It all seemed so unjust. But there was no point struggling now. Perhaps he'd find a way to convince the police of his innocence.

'Right! I want a couple of you to take him back to the station,' the Chief Squeaker said, addressing his men, 'while the rest of you maintain order here. Let the respectable gents on the towpath go about their lawful business, and keep a close eye on that ex-lawyer and his bunch of pirates. If any of them try to get off their ship . . . arrest them!' The Chief Squeaker winked at Snatcher.

'Here, sir!' he said as he handed the wings over. 'And if we can be of any more service to you?'

Snatcher turned the wings over in his hands, smiled, and turned to Arthur. 'I was wondering how we were going to put them back together. You have done us a service. There are a few questions I would like to ask you . . . ' Then he turned to the Chief Squeaker and spoke in a sly voice.

'I know how understaffed you are at the police station. I think it might be as well if you were to let me help you out by keeping the boy,' Snatcher smirked.

'No! You can't do that!' shouted Willbury from the deck.

'Oh yes I can!' replied the Chief Squeaker. He then placed a hand on Snatcher's shoulder.

'By the powers invested in me I now pronounce you a Temporary Gaoler Class 3. Please take custody of this criminal on behalf of the Ratbridge Police.'

Snatcher winked. 'Oh, certainly, Officer. Anything to help out the police!'

'Oi, you two! Grab him!' the new Temporary Gaoler Class 3 snapped to a couple of rather sorry looking Members.

The two approached Arthur. The older one was bandaged from waist to knee, while the younger one's nose was covered in sticking plaster.

*The older one was bandaged from waist to knee,
while the younger one's nose was covered in sticking plaster.*

'It's them!' Marjorie shouted from the deck. 'Those are the men who stole—'

The Chief Squeaker cut her off. 'Any more trouble from you lot, and I shall have you all locked up.'

Willbury grabbed Marjorie's arm.

'Yes. Any more trouble, and I'm sure the police will want to give us the power to administer punishment to our prisoner as well,' said Snatcher, eyeing Willbury.

'Quite right, sir,' responded the Chief Squeaker. 'It is so nice to find a co-operative member of the public like yourself.'

Snatcher then spoke to the Trouts. 'Take the boy back to the Cheese Hall!'

Arthur looked very nervously back at Willbury as he was led away. 'What am I going to do?' he cried. The thought of trying to escape from the Cheese Hall again filled him with despair. And what on earth would they do to him once they got him there?

'We will get you back!' called Willbury after him.

'I am sure your diligence will be well rewarded,' Snatcher smirked to the Chief Squeaker. 'I will arrange for some "paperwork" to be delivered to you later.'

'Oh, thank you, sir!'

The Chief Squeaker mounted his bicycle and set off down the towpath, leaving his men guarding the laundry.

The Chief Squeaker mounted his bicycle and set off down the towpath

Willbury and the crew stood in silence, watched by the policemen.

'Just when I thought things were getting better!'

muttered Willbury to himself. 'Poor Arthur—it was so brave of him to rescue the underlings and get his wings back. Now he's worse off than ever! What are we going to do?'

A Squeaker on guard

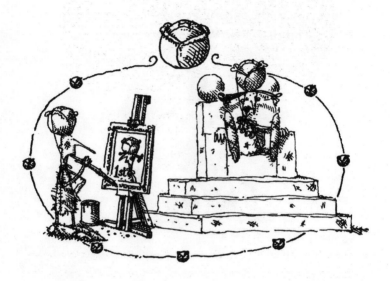

The queen very much enjoyed having her portrait painted, and would sit every two weeks for new sets of stamps. For those that couldn't read, the value of the stamp was defined by the size of cabbage she wore on her head.

*They assembled before the throne on the high
stone platform at the end of their cavern*

Chapter 12

Exodus

Back in the Underworld, all the remaining cabbageheads had
gathered together. They assembled before the throne on the
high stone platform at the end of their cavern. Below them
the floor of the cavern was now under several feet of water,
and the level was rising very quickly.

The queen adjusted the enormous cabbage on her head,
and then gave a haughty cough. She was the only
cabbagehead who ever spoke louder than a whisper. 'We
have brought you here today, for we have unfortunate
tidings to impart. Pursuant to the ever-rising levels of ill
commodious ablutive liquids, we believe sustainable brassica
production ceases to be feasible. Therefore I decree that
henceforth we must sojourn to an alternative affiliated
venue. Hey nonny nonny, we have spoken!'

A very old cabbagehead made his way up the steps to the throne

The other cabbageheads looked at each other, confused. None of them knew what she was talking about.

Then a very old cabbagehead made his way up the steps to the throne, and whispered in the queen's ear. She gave an embarrassed nod and spoke again.

'In alternative parlance, it is too wet to grow cabbages here any more, and we'll have to find somewhere else to grow them.'

There was a lot of nervous muttering amongst the cabbageheads.

The old cabbagehead whispered in the queen's ear once more. Then she spoke again.

''Tis brought to one's attention that vertically positioned below dales some few leagues beyond the confines of the above populace is a sufficient aperture that we may abide. Thus we might alight and henceforth meander to yonder aperture to re establish a harmonious intergraded monarchical community, and go forth with our troglodyte agriculture.'

There was more muttering from the 'common' cabbageheads, and the old cabbagehead once more spoke to the queen. She went a deeper red.

'There is another cave not far from here where we can move to and grow cabbages,' she said rather awkwardly.

A small cabbagehead approached the throne and whispered to the old cabbagehead. He in turn whispered to the queen, and she spoke again. 'It would appear that one's subjects that are currently absent from one's realm while . . . '

The old cabbagehead gave the queen a steely gaze and she started again.

'One . . . We need someone to go and find Titus and the others, and tell them where we've gone to.'

Two younger cabbageheads raised their hands.

Two younger cabbageheads raised their hands

'Very good,' said the queen. 'Now follow one, and one's assistant,' she said indicating the old man, 'and don't forget one's seeds!'

The crowd all patted their pockets and giggled. The old cabbagehead descended the steps, and led the crowd up a tunnel away from the platform.

The queen found herself sitting alone, and feeling rather disgruntled. She surveyed her kingdom of water and bobbing cabbages one last time, and then followed.

She surveyed her kingdom of water and bobbing cabbages one last time

THE DUNGEON UNDER THE CHEESE HALL

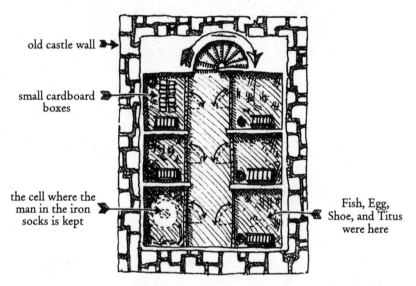

old castle wall ➤➤

small cardboard ➤➤
boxes

the cell where the ➤
man in the iron
socks is kept

Fish, Egg, ◄◄
Shoe, and Titus
were here

The dungeon under the laboratory has a long and gruesome history, and predates the Cheese Hall by hundreds of years. It was constructed in 1247 as the dungeon/torture chamber/nursery/food cellar/rubbish tip for Ratbridge castle. In 1453 revolting peasants destroyed the castle. Eight babies and three hardened criminals survived, trapped in the dungeon for two years before they were discovered by a team of local builders who were redeveloping the site as a shoe shop. For the next hundred years the dungeon was used as a storeroom for shoes and the equipment left over from the torturing came in handy for fitting shoes to those who lied about their shoe size.

During this period a small cheese shop was built next door, and due to foul and sharp practices, became very successful. When the shoe shop failed, it was bought up by the cheese shop owner and was used as a secret workshop where date-expired labels were filed off cheeses and new forged ones applied. The cheese shop became wholesalers and gained control of the cheese trade in the area. Other cheese traders had to become members of a cheese guild (set up by the wholesalers) to be allowed to trade, and the empire expanded.

In 1712 the Cheese Hall was built and a laboratory was built behind it to further the 'science' of adulteration. The dungeon was found to be useful for the storage of those that caused any problems for the cheese guild, and long-term storage of failed experiments.

In the dungeon the Members surrounded Arthur

Chapter 13

BACK BELOW THE CHEESE HALL

In the dungeon the Members surrounded Arthur.

'What are we going to do with you, my little thief?' asked Snatcher.

'I am not the thief!' snapped Arthur.

'Oh, yes, you are! You took my wings!'

'Those were my wings. You stole them from me in the first place.'

'That is as maybe, but they are mine now. And for all the grief you've caused me, I think pretty much everything of yours is as good as mine.' Snatcher looked at Arthur then spoke again. 'Search 'im!'

The Members descended on Arthur, and emptied his pockets.

'Not much here, guv!'

Then one of the Members noticed the bump under Arthur's shirt.

'He's got something up his jumper!'

'Get it!' ordered Snatcher.

Arthur tried to defend his doll with his cuffed hands, but he was overpowered, and the doll pulled from him.

'What have we here?' asked Snatcher. 'The little boy has got a little dolly!'

'Ahhhh!' scoffed the Members.

'The little boy has got a little dolly!'

Arthur looked worried and reached for the doll. Snatcher laughed and threw it on the floor.

'By the time I've finished with you, that dolly is going to look like your big brother.'

The Members laughed.

'What do you mean?' asked Arthur.

Snatcher laughed and threw it on the floor

'Haven't you guessed yet? Have you not realized why we are collecting big creatures and why only little creatures leave here? We is nicking their SIZE!' scoffed Snatcher.

Arthur froze. 'Size?'

'Yes!' Snatcher laughed. 'It so happens that we have come by a certain device . . . ' He stopped and winked at the Trouts, who were holding Arthur. ' . . . that can extract the size from things. All your little friends who came our way are now your even littler friends.'

Snatcher and the others now all burst out laughing.

'But what's the point in doing that?' Arthur asked.

'That is for us to know. It is part of our BIG plan.' There was more laughter. Then Snatcher's face changed, and his voice turned nasty. 'And if it was not for you, things might be progressing a lot faster. I needed them monsters you freed. Perhaps you might like to donate some of your size instead?'

Arthur did not reply.

'Yes. I thought that might shut you up. You've put a spanner in the works. Now we have to go and find a load more monsters to shrink!' snarled Snatcher. He turned to the Trouts. 'Throw him in a cell. We'll sort him out the next time we fire up the machine.' Then he smirked horribly. 'And next time I go out on a little selling trip, I am sure all the ladies will be falling over themselves to buy a miniature boy!' He looked directly at Arthur, put on a simpering face and spoke in the unmistakable tones of Madame Froufrou: 'I 'ave only one of zese little creatures, for sale to ze most fashionably rich lady of all!'

Arthur gaped. So that explained why Madame Froufrou had reminded him so strongly of Snatcher! It was just a disguise! Was this man behind everything sinister in the town?

Sniggering at the look on Arthur's face, the Trouts lifted Arthur, and threw him through the door of the cell that had contained the trotting badgers. Snatcher walked over and locked the door. Arthur noticed that the keys were now attached to his waistcoat by a heavy metal chain.

Arthur noticed that the keys were now attached to his waistcoat by a heavy metal chain

'When are we going to fire up the machine . . . ?' asked Gristle.

'The sooner the better,' replied Snatcher. 'But there is no point doing it just for the boy, we'll get some more monsters to put in it.'

'Does that mean we have to go down . . . below?' Gristle was looking very worried.

'Don't worry, Gristle. I am sure somebody will hold your hand.' Snatcher smirked. Arthur noticed the other Members were also looking worried.

A quick cup of tea

'I think a quick cup of tea is in order,' Snatcher said, then all the Members set off up the stairs leaving Arthur alone in the dungeon.

Arthur alone in the dungeon

The police had set up camp on the towpath

Kipper was standing with Tom on the deck watching the Squeakers

Chapter 14

THE STAND OFF

Back on the laundry there was a stand off. The police had set up camp on the towpath and the crew stood about looking very glum. They were running out of food. Normally the crew would have gone shopping late on market day (to pick up bargains), but with all the excitement yesterday they had forgotten, and now they were not allowed off the ship.

Kipper was standing with Tom on the deck watching the Squeakers who were tucking into egg and bacon that they were cooking over a fire they had started on the towpath. The smell of the bacon was wafting over the side of the laundry.

'This is torture!' muttered Kipper.

'I think they must be doing it to wind us up,' replied Tom.

*The Squeakers were tucking into egg and bacon
that they were cooking over a fire*

The boxtrolls were also becoming uneasy. They were sniffing the air and gurgling to each other. Fish moved slowly to the top of the gangplank and stared hard at the feasting Squeakers. One of the new boxtrolls joined Fish and was whispering something to him.

'I think I can feel my energy sapping away,' said Kipper. 'If I don't get something to eat soon I shall just fade away.'

Tom looked up at Kipper's belly. 'The chance of you fading away is pretty remote. It's us rats I am worried about. We have a very high metabolic rate, you know.' Tom stopped and tugged on Kipper's arm. Fish had started to move very slowly down the gangplank towards the bank.

'What's he doing?' whispered Tom.

Kipper didn't answer and they watched as Fish reached the bank and walked nonchalantly straight past the

Squeakers. The Squeakers looked up but seemed to pay the boxtroll almost no attention at all.

'Why don't they grab him?' whispered Tom under his breath.

Kipper watched as the Squeakers returned their full attention to the egg and bacon. 'It's Townsfolk. I think it must be that they hold underlings in such low regard that they just don't notice them.'

Fish had made his way a little further down the canal bank and was now waving to the other boxtrolls on deck to join him. A small procession of boxtrolls now marched down the gangplank, past the Squeakers (who hardly gave them a second glance), and joined Fish.

A small procession of boxtrolls

'Well, blow me!' muttered Tom. 'Where do you think they are off to?'

'Off to find themselves breakfast,' said Kipper sounding very sorry for himself. 'I wish I was an underling!'

About twenty minutes later, Willbury was sitting in the captain's cabin, and Titus was playing with the miniature cabbagehead by the window, when Titus gave a squeak. Willbury turned to see him looking out of the window. Willbury got up and joined him. Back along the towpath came the boxtrolls, and they were all carrying sacks.

'Oh no!' said Willbury. 'What's going on?'

He rushed up on deck to witness the boxtrolls walk straight past the policemen and up the gangplank.

Titus looking out of the window

Marjorie was up on deck and was watching. 'Good, isn't it?'

Willbury looked baffled.

'Them Squeakers don't pay them any attention,' explained Kipper. 'So used to thinking of them as nothing, they just don't seem to notice them.'

Fish and his group of friends emptied out their sacks. There in the middle of the deck was a large pile of cake, biscuits, treacle, boiled sweets, toffee, shortbread, pasties, anchovies, pickled onions, raspberry jam, and lemonade bottles. The crew's eyes lit up, and the pile soon disappeared under a crowd of bodies.

Willbury, however, looked slightly disapproving.

Fish and his group of friends emptied out their sacks

'You know that Titus and the other cabbageheads don't like this sort of food. Didn't you think to bring anything for them?'

The boxtrolls looked a little grumpy. Shoe picked up a small sack which was still lying beside him on the floor and threw it huffily forward. Willbury reached down and emptied it out to reveal a pile of fruit and vegetables. He smiled at the sulking boxtrolls.

'Thank you, that is very thoughtful of you. I'll take these down to the store room to keep them safe for later.'

Once he returned to the deck, Willbury stood a few feet away from the mêlée, watching the crew gorge themselves on the food. Marjorie joined him. She was tucking hungrily into a doughnut. 'Aren't you hungry?' she asked.

'How could I be hungry at a time like this?' Willbury looked very downcast.

'I have a dreadful feeling that this is all my fault!' Marjorie said.

'What do you mean?' asked Willbury.

Marjorie led Willbury away from the group. 'It's my invention. I think I know what has happened to it. I had an idea, but when the Trouts turned up with Snatcher, I knew. . . I just knew.'

'The Trouts?' said Willbury, looking puzzled.

'Didn't you see the men who had hold of Arthur?' asked Marjorie.

'No, I think I must have been concentrating on Arthur rather than the men who had hold of him.'

'It was the Trouts, I swear it. They looked pretty rough, but I am sure it was them.'

'So Snatcher has your invention?'

'Yes.'

'Are you sure?'

'Yes. It's all these little creatures.'

'What do you mean?'

'The invention that was stolen from me was a resizing machine,' whispered Marjorie.

'A RESIZING MACHINE!' Willbury was flabbergasted.

'Yes, I have discovered how to take the size out of one thing and put it into another. In the wrong hands it could be very dangerous . . . and I think it has definitely got into the wrong hands . . . ' Marjorie looked mournful.

'How does this machine operate?' asked Willbury.

Willbury was flabbergasted

'It consists of two parts. If you have two things of equal size, one side of the machine drains the size out of one thing and the other part of the machine pumps the size into the other thing,' Marjorie explained.

'Do you mean it shrinks one thing and makes the other thing bigger?' asked Willbury.

'Yes . . . exactly. And Snatcher and his mob have got hold of it. I don't know quite what they are doing with it, but I bet it's something rotten.'

Willbury thought to himself for a moment, and then spoke. 'Well, we know what they're doing with it. They're shrinking the underlings!'

'Do you mean it shrinks one thing and makes the other thing bigger?' asked Willbury

'Yes . . . but that's only half of it.' Marjorie paused. 'Where is all the size going?'

Willbury thought to himself then muttered, 'Oh my word! I hadn't thought of that.' Then he asked Marjorie another question.

'Why underlings?'

'It only works on living creatures. I guess they thought that nobody would notice or care if they used underlings.'

'Then I wonder why they have been blocking up the holes to the Underworld,' Willbury pondered. 'Surely that would stop the underlings coming above ground and falling into their clutches.'

'I've been thinking about that too. I think they must be blocking up the holes to help trap them in some way. Perhaps there is only one hole still open, and they lie in wait for the underlings there, knowing it is their only way to the surface . . . I don't know,' answered Marjorie.

'This is truly awful. Whatever possessed you to build a machine that could resize living creatures?'

Marjorie looked very embarrassed

'Truthfully?' Marjorie looked very embarrassed. 'I was interested in the scientific principles involved in making it. I just wanted to see if it was possible. I hadn't really worked out what it was going to be used for,' said Marjorie.

Then Willbury spoke again. 'I wonder what it is they are making bigger.'

'I don't rightly know. And I have been trying to work out how the cheese comes into it.'

'It must do somehow.' Willbury then spoke in a determined manner: 'I have a very bad feeling about this. We have to get Arthur back, and stop whatever is going on! Let's call a Council of War!'

The man in the iron socks

Against one wall was a bed

Chapter 15

THE MAN IN THE IRON SOCKS

Alone in the cold dank dungeon, Arthur looked around his cell. Against one wall was a bed. It had probably not been very comfortable even before it had been used by the trotting badgers, but now it was covered with bite marks, and he thought he would just get peppered with splinters if he tried to use it. Shreds of an old blanket had been used to form a kind of nest in one corner of the cell. This did not look very inviting either.

'I bet it's full of fleas!' Arthur muttered.

The only other things in the cell were a filthy bucket, and a few strands of straw scattered about the floor. Arthur walked to the bars and looked out. About six feet away lay his doll!

If I could reach it I could speak to Grandfather and he might be able to help me, thought Arthur.

The doll lay a few feet from his grasp

He lay on the floor and reached as far as he could. If only he could get the doll back. It lay a few feet from his grasp, almost as if it had been positioned deliberately to taunt him. He looked about his cell to see if there was anything he could use to help him. There was nothing.

'This is useless!' he moaned. Feeling completely at a loss, he got up and kicked the bed against the wall in frustration. After a second or so, there came a distant dull thump in return. Arthur was puzzled.

'What was that?'

He waited for a few moments but there were no more sounds, so he kicked the bed again. There was another thump. He didn't think it was an echo, but to be sure he kicked the bed twice in rapid succession. After a couple of seconds came a 'Thump! Thump! Thump!'

'It can't be an echo then!' He kicked the bed again . . . The thumping started again, but this time it didn't stop. Arthur pulled the bed from the wall, put his ear to the stonework, and listened. The thumping was coming from the next cell. There was definitely someone—or something—in there. Then Arthur realized that the cell next to him was the boarded-up cell of which the boxtrolls had been so frightened. He began to wish he hadn't attracted the attention of its occupant.

'Oh no! It sounds as if it's coming through!'

The thumping was getting louder and louder. Arthur looked down and noticed one of the bricks in the wall was moving out towards him.

'It is! It's coming through!' Arthur panicked. He jumped over the bed then smashed it as hard as he could against the wall, sending the brick shooting back in.

Someone shouted 'Ouch!' and the thumping stopped.

He jumped over the bed then smashed it as hard as he could against the wall

Arthur pulled the bed back again, and waited.

There was a muffled cry, an even louder thump, and, before Arthur had time to react again, the loose brick flew out of the wall and landed on the floor.

There was a slight pause, then a hand holding a stub of candle appeared through the hole. Arthur froze.

'What's all this noise about? Can't a prisoner get any sleep round here?' came a very grumpy voice. 'I'm the only one round here allowed to make a din.'

A face covered by a mask peered back

Arthur got down and peered into the hole. A face covered by a mask peered back.

'Who are you?' asked Arthur.

'I am Herbert!' came the reply. 'And who are you? You are not one of these Cheese Wallahs are you? Can't stand cheese or anything to do with it! Used to love it, but you can have too much of a good thing!'

'No. My name is Arthur,' said Arthur.

'Where you from?' said Herbert curtly. 'And what are you doing here?'

'I am from the Underworld. But I've got stuck up here in Ratbridge, and now I've been caught and put in this cell.'

'Blimey. You're in for it. I've heard what they is up to. Blooming evil! You is going to get shrunk!'

Arthur peered through the hole.

'Did you make this hole?'

'Course I did! I make lots of holes. Trouble is that when I do it makes so much noise that the Cheese Wallahs always come and fill them in again. Never seems to get me anywhere. Been trying to get out of here for years, but never been lucky. If I could get these socks off they wouldn't be able to hold me.'

'Socks?' asked Arthur.

'Yes. The Cheese Wallahs shoved me into a pair of iron socks to slow me down. They still don't dare come too close!'

'The Cheese Wallahs shoved me into a pair of iron socks to slow me down'

'Why is that?'

'They is scared of me, what with me mask and me walloper. I made me a mask out of a bit of my old boots, and a big walloper out of me bed, and if they come near me . . . wallop!'

'What's a walloper?'

'It's me big mallet! It's great for all kinds of walloping. I love it!'

'You wallop them with it?'

'I wallop everything with it!'

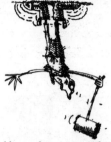

'So if I cause any trouble . . . they just turn the magnet on . . . boink!'

'I wallop everything with it! Trouble is the Cheese Wallahs got tired of it, and fixed up a way of stopping me walloping them.'

'How?'

'They stuck these socks on me and a huge electro-magnet in the ceiling above my cell, so if I cause any trouble . . . they just turn the magnet on . . . boink! I stick to the ceiling. Blooming iron socks!'

'Is that painful?' asked Arthur.

'Only when they turn the magnet off! I drops to the floor, you see . . . Bonk! But I still usually manage to wallop one or two of them.'

'Why are you locked up here?' Arthur enquired.

'Me? Can't remember much now 'cause it's been such a long, long time. Something to do with me and . . . ' Herbert's voice trailed off.

'How long have you been here?'

'Can't rightly say. But I know that I have walloped more than a hundred and thirty of them over the years!'

'A hundred and thirty!' declared Arthur.

'Well, some of them might be the same person I walloped a few times. It was much easier in the early days before they put me in the socks. These days I am lucky to get even one of them!'

'Do you know what they are up to?'

'Well, I know they are shrinking underlings what they trap and steal,' replied Herbert. 'Don't know why.'

'You say that they're trapping underlings?' asked Arthur.

'Yes, I heard them talking about it when they brought some in. They got some kind of way down into the Underworld . . . and they set traps.'

Arthur's interest was growing. 'What do you know about how they get into the Underworld?'

'Not much! But I think they must have some way down from 'ere at the Cheese Hall, 'cause it don't take 'em long.'

Arthur's mind began to whirr. If there was a route between the Cheese Hall and the Underworld then maybe there was a way for him to get back to Grandfather after all. If only he could get hold of his doll and tell Grandfather what he had learned, perhaps they could come up with a plan.

If only he could get hold of his doll and tell Grandfather what he had learned

Snatcher climbed on to a table and took a look out
through the boards that covered the tearoom windows

'You worry too much.'

Chapter 16

GOING DOWN!

Snatcher climbed on to a table and took a look out through the boards that covered the tearoom windows. It was raining again.

'Well, is it raining?' asked Gristle.

'No!' Snatcher lied, and climbed back down off the table.

'I still don't like it. It's getting very wet down there. Last time we were up to our knees in water.'

'You worry too much.' Snatcher chortled at the nervous-looking Members assembled before him. They didn't look convinced. 'One more load of them monsters and a few more cheeses, and all will be tickety-boo for our plans for Ratbridge.'

'The traps were nearly empty on the last two trips.'

'I know,' said Snatcher. 'Why else do yer think I got yer to grab them rats, and monsters from the shop? Now get on

'Last time we were up to our knees in water'

with yer!' Snatcher fixed Gristle with his good eye. 'Or perhaps I could come up with a substitute for monsters . . . If you get my drift?'

Gristle turned pale. 'No . . . er . . . I'm sure we can find something in the traps.'

'Very good. Just make sure you do!' said Snatcher. 'The Great One needs 'em, and we need the Great One. Our plan relies on 'im. If you get a good haul, this will be the last time, and after that we can seal up the Underworld completely.'

'Promise?'

'Promise!'

The Members looked happier.

'All right then!' said Snatcher as he walked over to a large cupboard and opened its doors. 'First trapping party inside!'

A small group of the Members carrying sacks walked forward, and reluctantly entered the cupboard. Snatcher gave them a wink and closed the doors. Then he took hold of a bell pull next to the cupboard.

*A small group of the Members carrying sacks walked
forward, and reluctantly entered the cupboard*

'Going down!' he giggled, and pulled the bell pull. There
was a grinding noise, then muffled screams that faded away.
After a couple of seconds there was a distant splash, followed
by a bell ping.

'Maybe it is a little wet,' Snatcher smirked. Then he
waited for a few seconds before pulling the bell pull again.
After a few more seconds there was another ping, and
Snatcher opened the doors. The cupboard was empty, apart
from two inches of dirty water that ran out onto the carpet.

'Second trapping party, please,' ordered Snatcher.

The Members looked very, very nervous and shuffled
backwards.

*The cupboard was empty, apart from two inches
of dirty water that ran out onto the carpet*

'Second trapping party, PLEASE!' Snatcher snapped.

Reluctantly, the remaining group walked into the cupboard.

'Not you, Gristle!' Snatcher said. 'You can go down on the last load with me.' He closed the cupboard and sent the Members on their way. Then he turned to Gristle and took a banknote out of his pocket. 'But first I want you to pop down the shops quick and get me a pair of wellies.'

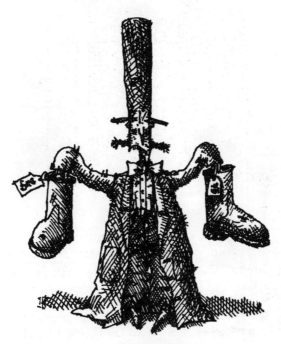

Gristle with wellies

Kipper and Tom disturb the meeting in the hold

Willbury, Marjorie, and the captain sat behind an ironing board

Chapter 17

THE COUNCIL OF WAR

It was early evening and it was raining . . . again. In the hold of the laundry all the dirty clothes had been pushed to one end to make space for the Council of War. Willbury, Marjorie, and the captain sat behind an ironing board, facing the crew and underlings. Even Match and the miniature cabbagehead and fresh-water sea-cow were there. The fresh-water sea-cow had been adopted by some of the crew and was swimming about in a small barrel on wheels amongst her new guardians, who kept sneaking her lumps of cucumber. The only people missing were Kipper, Tom . . . and Arthur.

Willbury looked about, and then turned to the captain. 'Where are Kipper and Tom?'

'We needed someone to act as watch on deck, and as it was raining, I gave them the duty as punishment. They should never have let Arthur go into the Cheese Hall alone.'

The fresh-water sea-cow had been adopted by some of the crew

'Oh . . . all right . . . Well, I think we'd better call the meeting to order, and get started.' Willbury stood up, and the hold fell quiet.

'My friends, we have a number of problems. Firstly, we have to get Arthur back from the Cheese Guild and return him to his grandfather. And secondly, I think we must find out what Snatcher is up to, and put an end to it.' Willbury paused. 'I have some disturbing new information. Snatcher, we think, is in possession of a new invention.'

Marjorie looked uncomfortable and stared at the floor.

'It is a machine that resizes things!'

There were gasps from the crowd.

'Yes! I believe it is Snatcher and his mob that are responsible for the tininess of our tiny friends.'

Match and the little cabbagehead who were standing on a stepladder amongst the underlings squeaked, and they all turned to look.

'We don't know what he is doing with the size he takes from the creatures—but I think we can be pretty certain that whatever it is, we're not going to like it. We have to get into the Cheese Hall. Does anybody have any ideas?'

Match and the little cabbagehead were standing on a stepladder

Willbury looked around expectantly, but there was no reply.

The meeting in the hold had been almost silent for two minutes, and Willbury was trying to decide what to do next, when Tom and Kipper suddenly burst through the door, drenched from the rain on deck.

'Willbury!' cried Tom as he and Kipper scanned the surprised faces. 'We've just spotted some cabbageheads on the towpath! Two of them! What should we do?'

'We've just spotted some cabbageheads on the towpath!'

'Hmm,' said Willbury. 'I wonder where they have come from—all the cabbageheads from the Cheese Hall are down here with us, aren't they, Titus?'

Titus nodded, looking excited.

'Then I think you had better go up and see what's happening, Titus.'

Titus stood and made his way quickly past Tom and Kipper and up the stairs to the deck. Tom and Kipper followed, along with the other cabbageheads and Willbury.

As soon as he reached the deck, Titus ran to the side of the ship and disappeared down the gangplank.

He ran past the Squeakers and along the towpath till he approached the shadows where Tom and Kipper had seen the cabbageheads. The others watched from the deck as shapes in the shadows approached Titus and seemed to be having a conversation. Then Titus turned back towards the laundry, followed by two other cabbageheads. They looked very nervous and were holding hands. Titus led them past the Squeakers, who ignored them completely, and up the gangplank.

Titus turned back towards the laundry, followed by two other cabbageheads

As soon as they reached the deck the cabbageheads all ran to meet each other, hugged, and started whispering. After a few minutes the huddle broke up, and Titus came over to

The cabbageheads all ran to meet each other

Willbury, looking quite agitated. Willbury leant over to allow Titus to whisper in his ear. When Titus had finished whispering, Willbury stood upright and spoke.

'Oh dear me! The cabbageheads have all fled from their home. It seems that the water level underground has driven them out.'

'How did they get up here if the holes are all blocked?' asked Kipper.

Willbury looked puzzled. 'That is an excellent question. I . . . or rather Titus . . . shall have to ask them.'

Titus scampered over to where the cabbageheads stood, and they formed another huddle. After a few moments he returned and whispered in Willbury's ear again. Willbury turned back towards the others with an expression of surprise on his face.

'They came up through the rabbit women's tunnels. Arthur told me about the tunnels, but he didn't know quite

where they were. Apparently they come up in the woods just
outside town.'

Kipper smiled. 'Well, that's how we get into the Cheese
Hall then. We get under the town and burrow up!'

Tom and Willbury turned to look at Kipper.

'They came up through the rabbit women's tunnels'

'You're right, Kipper! You're not as green as you are—
No, that would not be very apppropriate,' said Willbury.
'Titus, would your friends show us the way?'

Titus returned to the new cabbageheads and whispered to
them. They nodded.

' . . . But how do we get off the boat?' asked Tom. He
looked across at the Squeakers, who were still drinking tea
and looking very wet and grumpy. Any attempt to get off
this laundry by the crew was going to be noticed.

'I just don't know . . . ' said Willbury. 'Why don't we go
back down to the meeting, tell them about the tunnels, and
get out of this rain? There has to be a way to get past the
Squeakers.'

The Squeakers were still drinking tea and looking very wet and grumpy

Tom and Kipper looked sheepish. 'We are supposed to stay up here and keep watch.'

Willbury smiled. 'I don't think anybody is going to attack us in this rain. Why don't you come down with us?'

They went below. Willbury returned to his chair, and the others found space amongst the underlings. The captain and the others looked quizzically at the newcomers.

Willbury spoke. 'Gentlemen, the cabbageheads who have joined us have just come up from the Underworld. They have found tunnels that are not blocked, which come up just outside the town walls, in the woods. Kipper has suggested that we use these tunnels to get under the town and burrow up into the Cheese Hall.'

There were murmurings of approval, and Willbury turned and smiled at Kipper.

'It's going to take a lot of burrowing,' said Bert.

'Yes . . . yes, it is,' said Willbury. 'I think we'll need as many hands and paws as we can muster. Volunteers?'

A sea of hands and paws went up, and was followed by a cheer.

'Good. But we have a major problem. How do we get off the laundry?' asked Willbury.

'We could jump over the side and tie up the Squeakers, then throw them in the drink!' said Bert.

*'We could jump over the side and tie up the
Squeakers, then throw them in the drink!'*

There was another cheer.

'I don't think so, Bert. There are rather a lot of policemen, and they might win in a fight. Even if they didn't, if even one of them got away, he could warn the Cheese Guild we were coming.'

They all sat and thought.

'Boxtrolls!' Kipper cried.

'What do you mean, boxtrolls?' asked Willbury with a puzzled look on his face.

'Seeing that the boxtrolls and cabbageheads can get on and off the ship, we dress up as boxtrolls. Then the Squeakers won't pay any attention to us.'

'You don't think the Squeakers might notice we're not real boxtrolls?' asked the captain.

'Well, they're not too bright,' said Tom.

'And if the disguises were good then I think we might get away with it,' smiled Willbury.

'Don't you think that they'd notice if there was no one left on the ship?' asked the captain.

'I think that we might be able to get around that,' said Marjorie. 'Leave it to me.'

Soon everybody was busy. In a storeroom, where the crew kept all the things that they would put out for recycling, were a lot of folded up cardboard boxes. Under the guidance of Fish and the other boxtrolls, the crew prepared these. They found that economy Stainpurge boxes were just about the right size for humans, and that luxury 'Blotch-b-white' boxes fitted the rats. Meanwhile the rats set about making troll teeth out of the vegetables and fruit, while Marjorie was seen constructing dummies and some strange rigging device out of ropes and laundry. By late that evening everybody was below decks and ready. Fish and the other boxtrolls were very happy having so many new 'boxtrolls' about, and were chortling to themselves.

Willbury raised his hands and shushed the crowd. Then he spoke. 'Arr arware bawaee waaee.'

Soon everybody was busy

'Whaa?' came the reply.

Willbury took out his new orange-peel teeth.

'I said, is everybody ready?' There was a lot of nodding
and giggling. 'Well then, I think it may be best if we leave the
laundry in ones and twos, then meet up by the West Gate.
If we take a rope ladder we can use it to climb down from the
town wall.'

Tom found a rope ladder and Kipper stowed it inside his
new box. With his new parsnip teeth Kipper looked like
Fish's bigger brother.

'Is your distraction ready?' Willbury asked Marjorie.

Marjorie nodded. 'I have arranged a party . . . powered by
the beam engine, for the policemen to watch. It's going to
take a few minutes to really get going, but I don't see why we
can't start sneaking off. It should stop them noticing that the
ship is empty.'

The captain and Willbury organized everybody and handed out candles. These would be needed in the dark tunnels. Then they led the first group up onto the deck.

Marjorie followed them up the stairs. The 'boxtrolls' then started to make their way down the gangplank in small groups, and walked straight past the policemen.

On deck Marjorie adjusted the beam engine and the flywheel started to turn. She'd piped some of the steam from the boiler to a small harmonium and the crows had agreed to stay behind, as they were not very good at burrowing, and play the instrument. As their beaks hit the keys, steam and a great deal of noise started to come from the back of the keyboard. The crows were delighted. Before long terrible tunes could be heard up and down the towpath. The Squeakers covered their ears and moaned.

As their beaks hit the keys, steam and a great deal of noise started to come from the back of the keyboard

'It's working!' said Marjorie.

She pulled a handle on the side of the beam engine and a number of ropes fixed to pulleys tightened. Strange cloth figures appeared, and started to dance about the deck. The Squeakers were straining their necks to see the dancers but they were obviously unwilling to get too close to the awful noise, and did not approach the boat. More boxtrolls made their way up on deck and sauntered past the police, unnoticed. After half an hour only Marjorie and Willbury were left on board.

Strange cloth figures appeared, and started to dance about the deck

'This is really ingenious, Marjorie. I hope it will give us the time we need!' Willbury said.

Marjorie looked a little sad. 'It's the least I can do to help. I still feel terrible that my invention has caused so much trouble. I'll do anything to put things right.'

'You mustn't blame yourself,' said Willbury kindly. 'You had no way of knowing what would happen. All we can do is

to do our best to thwart these awful people, and stop whatever it is they're up to. Now, I think it's time for us to go. How long will this dancing, and "music" last?'

'Well, if the crows can keep stoking the boiler, it could go on all night.' Marjorie smiled.

'I don't think that will be very popular with the locals!' said Willbury.

'You never know. The crows might get better!' Marjorie chuckled. They put their teeth in and set off.

The West Gate

When Willbury and Marjorie arrived at the
West Gate, Tom rushed up to meet them

Chapter 18

UP AND UNDER!

When Willbury and Marjorie arrived at the West Gate, Tom rushed up to meet them, and snatched his teeth out of his mouth so he could talk.

'Quick! Bert has just seen town guards. They're coming round on their patrol, and they'll be here in a minute.'

Willbury took out his boxtroll teeth. 'They won't bother us if we are dressed as boxtrolls, will they?'

'Yes they will! They're not like the police—they're always on the lookout for boxtrolls. They know who's responsible for "borrowing" things. They hate them!' replied Tom.

'Let's get over the wall then,' suggested Willbury.

Tom looked up at the town wall. 'How?'

Willbury followed his gaze. 'Oh my. We didn't work that out, did we!'

'We've got to do something,' Tom said urgently.

'I ah . . . ah.' Willbury started to panic. Then he felt a tapping on his box. It was Fish.

Fish pointed at the real boxtrolls who were settling themselves outside a sweetshop that stood next to the wall. They crouched down, then pulled their heads and arms inside the boxes. All that was left was what appeared to be a pile of boxes outside the shop. Fish led Willbury over to the shop and indicated to him to do the same.

'Fish wants us to pretend to be boxes. Quick! Do as he says!' Willbury whispered to the others.

With the help of Fish they assembled themselves in a stack outside the shop. Fish settled down beside them, and the cabbageheads hid behind the stack. Footsteps approached.

Fish pointed at the real boxtrolls who were settling themselves outside a sweetshop

'An' I sez to 'er, if our girl Sonya did that to . . . 'Ello? What we got here?' said a voice.

'Looks like someone has made a late delivery to the sweetshop,' said the second. 'They wasn't 'ere an hour ago.'

The two guards approached the boxes. One of them rubbed his chin and looked about.

The two guards approached the boxes

'I am rather partial to sweets. Mind you, "Stainpurge" doesn't sound that tasty. Still, you never know . . . Do yer think anyone is going to miss one of these boxes?'

'No! Course not! There must be at least twenty or thirty of them and if one goes missing that's only five per cent! You must expect five per cent natural wastage when you leave something lying about, don't you think?'

'Oh, I should think so! Do you think that if we got a cart, then maybe twenty or thirty per cent natural wastage might be acceptable?'

'I should think that if we got my brother Big Alf's wagon, then almost a hundred per cent natural wastage might occur!'

'You stay here and I'll get the wagon!'

Off went one of the guards while the other kept watch on the stack of boxes. After a few minutes there was a clattering of wheels. A large, high wagon appeared, stopped by the wall, and the guard jumped down. With difficulty the two of them managed to lift the boxes onto the wagon. When their backs were turned the cabbageheads jumped up, and hid amongst the boxes now on the wagon. When the guards had finished they stopped for a breather.

A large, high wagon appeared

A head popped out of one of the larger boxes and looked about. It was Willbury. He saw that the top of the town wall was just inches above him, and he smiled. A hand came out from the side of his box, and removed his troll teeth.

'RIGHT! Everybody over the wall!' he shouted.

The two guards looked round and fainted at the sight of a cart-load of boxes all standing up at the same time.

They all clambered on to the top of the wall from the cart, and Kipper got out the rope ladder, hooked it to the top of the wall, and lowered it over the other side. Climbing down

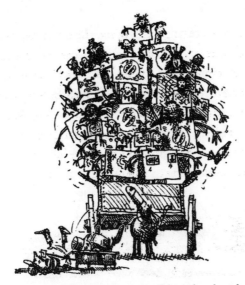

*The two guards looked round and fainted at the sight
of a cart-load of boxes all standing up at the same time.*

dressed in a cardboard box was not easy and several of the
pirates ended up dropping off the ladder and crumpling their
boxes. This distressed the real boxtrolls.

When everybody was down, Titus whispered in
Willbury's ear.

'We'll follow our cabbagehead friends—they'll lead us to
the rabbit women's tunnels,' said Willbury. The party set off
following the new cabbageheads. It made a strange sight,
with the moon casting long shadows across the landscape.

Soon they were in the woods. The new cabbageheads wandered about a bit before they found an old oak tree. They ran to its base and pulled back some undergrowth to reveal a large hole between the tree's roots. Everybody gathered round as the new cabbageheads whispered to Titus. Titus then whispered to Willbury and after some moments Willbury spoke to the group.

'This is the entrance to the rabbit women's tunnels. Our new cabbagehead friends don't want to go any further.' Willbury smiled at the cabbageheads. 'They are rather frightened of what's happening down there, and want to catch up with the other cabbageheads who are apparently making their way to a new cave in the hills. I think it is totally understandable. We don't really know what we are going to find down there.'

They ran to its base and pulled back some undergrowth to reveal a large hole between the tree's roots

There were some nervous murmurings from the crowd.

'Yes, I think we should thank them for bringing us this far.'

The new cabbageheads looked rather chuffed, and gave a little bow. Titus approached Willbury again. When he'd finished Willbury spoke.

'Titus says that the cabbageheads that Arthur freed are going to go with them, but that he himself would like to stay with us for the moment and help to find Arthur.' Willbury turned to Titus. 'You are very brave, Titus.'

The murmurings in the crowd grew louder, and Titus took Fish's hand. The other cabbageheads took one last look at the hole, waved and disappeared rapidly into the woods.

The other cabbageheads disappeared rapidly into the woods

The strange party stood around the hole

The captain lit his candle

Chapter 19

THE RABBIT WOMEN

The strange party stood around the hole. It was much, much larger than a rabbit hole, but it would still be a tight fit for a large pirate dressed in a stiff cardboard box. There was an air of trepidation among the group—if the cabbageheads were so frightened of what they would find down the hole, was it really a place that the rest of them wanted to go?

'Who is going to lead the way?' asked Willbury.

There was a pause. Then Fish and Titus put up their free hands.

'Very well,' said Willbury. 'Everybody get out your candles.'

The captain walked over to the hole, produced a box of matches, and lit his candle.

'Right then, me hearties!' he said. 'Form an orderly queue!'

Everybody got in line, with Fish and Titus at the front, followed by Willbury, Tom, Kipper, and Marjorie. Then, one by one, each member of the queue took a light from the captain's candle and disappeared down the hole. Some of the larger pirates took quite a bit of shoving to get them into the hole, but they were all able to manage it without damaging their boxes.

Once underground the tunnel opened out, and even Kipper could stand up and move about with ease. There was a warm earthy smell in the passage.

The procession set off. After a few hundred yards Fish held up a hand, and the procession ground to a stop. Fish turned to Willbury and put his finger to his lips. Then Titus whispered something to Willbury, and Willbury turned to Kipper and Tom.

Even Kipper could stand up and move about with ease

'Fish wants us all to be quiet, and Titus wants us to put our teeth in. Pass it along.'

The message passed down the line, and soon all that could be heard was the sound of teeth being put in. Fish and Titus put their candles down and disappeared into the darkness.

'Aat oo ooh iiink aaye rrr oooht ooo?' Kipper whispered.

'Iiierrrt!' snapped Tom.

After a minute or two, they heard voices from somewhere ahead. The voices grew louder and small green lights appeared. Before long Willbury could make out Fish, Titus, and some other shapes coming towards them.

As they got closer, the candlelight revealed that Fish and Titus had returned with two rabbit women. The women were both dressed in knitted one-piece suits, with long ears, and they carried glass jars full of glow-worms.

The women were both dressed in knitted one-piece suits, with long ears, and they carried glass jars full of glow-worms

They marched up to Willbury and smiled.

One of them, in a grey suit, spoke. 'Your friend Titus has told us that you'd like us to guide you through our tunnels so you can get under Ratbridge?'

Willbury nodded.

Then the other, who was dressed in brown, spoke. 'We'll show you the way but you'll have to be very careful.'

Willbury nodded again, and the rabbit women smiled. Then the one in brown gave Kipper a funny look.

'You look rather big for a boxtroll.' Then she looked down at Tom. 'And you look rather small?'

Titus trotted over to her and whispered.

'What's he say, Coco?' asked the rabbit woman in the grey suit.

'Well, Fen, he says they're a different type of boxtroll . . . just visiting.'

'Well, that explains it!'

'I suppose so. But I think they need to see a dentist.'

Willbury blushed.

'Come this way, please, and please remember to be careful!' The rabbit women led the way.

After a short walk the tunnel became lighter, and Willbury could hear more voices. They rounded a bend and were confronted by a wooden door. In the centre of the door was a notice.

A wooden door

Please close the door after you.
Remember
There are trotting badgers about, and
we don't want to lose any of the old folks!

'Mind where you walk!' warned Coco, and then she opened the door.

Through the door was a large, low cavern. Hundreds of jam jars, filled with glow-worms, were tied to roots that hung from the ceiling, and a pale green light fell on the scene below. There were small groups of rabbit women working at looms and spinning wheels, and tending raised vegetable beds. All around them were thousands of rabbits. By each group of workers sat a rabbit woman reading aloud.

There were small groups of rabbit women working at looms and spinning wheels, and tending raised vegetable beds

Fen turned and spoke. 'Please be very careful not to step on our parents. They are not very bright, but we do love them.'

As the group carefully made their way through the door and into the cavern, Willbury noticed Marjorie was grinning from ear to ear despite her vegetable teeth. She was obviously

very impressed by the rabbit women. As Fen closed the door behind them after shooshing some rabbits away, Marjorie made her way to Willbury, and furtively removed her teeth.

'They're fantastic,' she whispered. 'Just who are they?'

Willbury checked to see that nobody was watching and slipped his teeth out. 'The story I heard was that they were abandoned babies or little girls that fell down rabbit holes. The rabbits took them in and brought them up as their own. It seems to make sense. I guess as they grew up they took charge and now look after the rabbits.'

Despite the working rabbit women not seeming to pay any attention to the visitors, Willbury and Marjorie both quickly put their teeth back in.

Coco pointed to the vegetable plots. 'We can grow most things here, but we avoid greens. Sometimes the old folks manage to burrow into the plots, and if they eat greens it doesn't agree with them.'

Fen noticed Willbury looking at the readers.

'We are very fond of books. You can learn nearly everything from them that rabbits can't teach you.'

Willbury was dying to take his teeth out again and ask questions, but he didn't want to give away that he was not a boxtroll. So as they were led through the cavern he listened and tried to make out what was being read. There were some passages from *The Country Housewife's Garden*, some Greek, mathematics, and even bits of *Tristram Shandy* and Jane Austen.

These rabbit women are very well educated! he thought.

The procession reached a door at the far side of the cavern and their guides led them through it and then closed it behind them.

'We are very fond of books. You can learn nearly everything from them that rabbits can't teach you.'

'We do have to be so careful as we have a real problem with trotting badgers. Last month someone left this door open, and Madeline's step-parents escaped and were eaten. It was very upsetting,' said Coco.

'It's all to do with the size of the tunnels,' added Fen. 'We had no idea when we made them bigger that it would allow the trotting badgers to get down them.'

They followed the rabbit women through a maze of passages till finally they reached one that tilted down at a steep angle. The passage emerged in a stone cave and the rabbit women halted. The floor of the cave was awash with water.

Coco held her jar aloft

Coco held her jar aloft.

'It's getting higher!' said Fen.

'Yes, but it will have to rise a good deal further before it gets close to our burrows. It's the cabbageheads and you boxtrolls that I am worried about.' Coco gave them a concerned look. Then she pointed into the darkness.

'At the other end of this cave is a tunnel that takes you under the town. I am sure Titus and your friend Fish can lead you from here.'

Willbury smiled through his vegetable teeth and bowed in thanks. The others followed his lead.

'No problem. And good luck,' said Coco, and she and Fen turned back up the passage and disappeared. When they had gone Willbury held up his candle, looked towards the other end of the cave, and took out his teeth.

'Fish and Titus, are you all right leading us from here?'

Fish took a very long smell at the air, smiled, and then nodded.

A rabbit woman gardening underground

Herbert and Arthur

'Do you think you could lend me your walloper?'

Chapter 20

THE DOLL

Back in the dungeon, Arthur was determined to find a way of escaping.

'Do you think you could lend me your walloper?' he asked the hole in the wall.

'You! Borrow my walloper! I should think not!' snapped Herbert. 'Anyway, what do you want it for?'

Arthur pleaded. 'A doll that I need is in the corridor outside the cell and I can't reach it. I need something to help me get it back.'

'Well, you can't borrow my walloper,' replied Herbert.

'Have you got anything else I could use?' asked Arthur.

'Might have!' Herbert was not an easy man. 'What's in it for me?'

Arthur thought for a moment. 'If I can get the doll, it might help me find a way out of here. And if I get out, I'll see if I can get you out as well.'

There was silence for a few moments then Herbert replied, 'Is a bit of string any good?'

Arthur looked across at the doll. 'It might be. How long is it?'

'About six feet.'

'That ought to do it.'

'Well, how much do you want to borrow?'

'Enough!' snapped Arthur in frustration.

'Well, would two feet do?'

'No!' barked Arthur. 'If you want to get out of here why don't you just lend me all of it?'

'Oh, all right! But don't get funny with me. It is my string!' came back a very grudging voice.

There was a scuffling in the cell beyond the hole and a ball of hairy string appeared

There was a scuffling in the cell beyond the hole and a ball of hairy string appeared. Arthur took it and said, 'Thank you.' Then he unwound it, tied a lasso in one end, and walked over to the bars. After a few attempts he managed to get the lasso around one of the doll's arms and hoist it into the cell.

'I've got it!' he cried.

'Can I have my string back?' came a worried voice from the hole.

*After a few attempts he managed to get the lasso around
one of the doll's arms and hoist it into the cell*

Arthur un-knotted the lasso, rolled up the string, and
held it out towards the hole. Herbert's hand darted out and
snatched it from him.

Arthur sat on the edge of his bed, and wound the handle
on the doll.

'Grandfather! Grandfather! Are you there?' he called.

There was a popping, some static noise, and then he heard
what he was hoping for.

'Arthur, where are you?'

'I am locked up in a cell below the Cheese Hall.'

'WHAT!' cried Grandfather. 'They caught you?'

'No,' said Arthur. 'I escaped . . . but the police handed
me over to Snatcher. He accused me of stealing the wings
from him!'

'Archibald Snatcher!' Grandfather sounded angry. 'He's
up to his old tricks again.'

'I am sorry, Grandfather.'

'You're not to blame. With that shyster involved nobody
is safe,' his grandfather said. 'We have to get you out of there
. . . and soon. Are you on your own?'

'Well, almost. There is a man called Herbert in the next cell.'

'Pardon? Did you say a man called Herbert?' asked Grandfather, sounding astonished.

'Yes!' said Arthur.

'Ask him if his nickname is Parsley!'

Arthur leant down to the hole and spoke. 'Is your nickname Parsley?'

'Don't you know it's rude to call your elders by their nicknames?' came the voice from the hole.

'That's him all right,' came Grandfather's voice. 'Arthur, can you let me speak to Herbert?'

Arthur held the doll out close to the hole, and he saw the masked eyes staring at it.

Arthur held the doll out close to the hole,
and he saw the masked eyes staring at it

'What are you doing there, Parsley?'

There was a silence from the hole, then Herbert's voice asked in a quizzical tone, 'Is that you, William?'

'Yes!'

'What are you doing talking out of a doll?'

'I will tell you later, but you . . . Oh, Herbert, I can't believe it's you. Are you all right? Have you been in that dungeon for all these years?'

'I . . . ' Herbert's voice trailed off. 'I . . . can't remember . . . '

'Herbert. Have you been in here all these years?'

'I am not sure. I am not even sure where I know you from . . . William . . . '

'Oh, Herbert. Don't you remember what happened?'

'No. Not really. My mind is so fuzzy.'

'Don't you remember the fight?'

'No . . . just something vaguely about you, me, and . . . Archibald Snatcher . . . it's all very confused.'

'Maybe if I remind you?' came Grandfather's voice.

'Maybe . . . ' muttered Herbert.

Arthur's grandfather paused for a moment. 'Arthur, you should listen to this too. It's time you heard the truth about why we live underground.'

'My mind is so fuzzy'

WHAT HAPPENS NEXT ...

The trouble continues for Arthur in book 3, *Cheese Galore!*
And time is running out both above and below ground.
Can Arthur and his friends summon up all their cunning
and save Ratbridge—and themselves?

Read the next gripping instalment of *Here Be Monsters!* to
discover the answers to all these questions and more ...

Why do Arthur and
Grandfather live
underground?

Will Willbury and the
others be able to rescue
Arthur from his cell?

What is the truth about
the secret goings-on in
the Cheese Hall?

Can Arthur and his friends think of a way of outwitting the dastardly Snatcher?

And just what is so important about some oil of Brussels,

some ladies with very large buttocks,

Herbert's walloper . . .

and a single cream bun?

Book 3,
Cheese Galore!,
available now
ISBN 978-0-19-275542-1